STYLE IS THE ROCKET

Books by Tom Simon

Lord Talon's Revenge

The Worm of the Ages and Other Tails

Death Carries a Camcorder and Other Essays

Writing Down the Dragon and Other Essays

THE EYE OF THE MAKER
The End of Earth and Sky
The Grey Death (forthcoming)

Visit the author's website at
bondwine.com

STYLE IS THE ROCKET
and Other Essays on Writing

by

TOM SIMON

Calgary
BONDWINE BOOKS
2016

Edited by Robin Eytchison
Editorial consultant: Wendy S. Delmater
Cover design by Sarah Huntrods

Published by Bondwine Books
ISBN 978-0-9952154-1-2

TABLE OF CONTENTS

PREFACE

In this, my third book of informal *essais,* I gather some pieces in which I tried to tackle points of style and substance in fiction writing. Occasionally I write with one eye on the market, as in 'Heinlein's rules' and 'Clock share'. But this is not a book about *selling* your writing; that I leave to persons who are qualified to write about it.

These pieces were written over the course of many years, and not everything in them is still current; but I have tried to choose items of some lasting value, and I hope that most of what I have had to say will still be of interest. The oldest piece, 'Sturgeon's Law School', was written in 2003; the newest, 'Quality *vs* quality', was written just a few weeks ago, especially for this book.

If I had to 'pot' the subject of this book in a phrase, I would probably channel Aristotle or Aquinas, and say that it is about distinguishing 'accidents' from 'essences' in fiction. A beautiful or ornamental style is an accident, in the philosophical sense: it is nice to have (within limits), but you can do without it at a pinch. A good story is essential. In 'Ozamataz' and 'Legosity', particularly, I examine some elements that have made some of the greatest stories so widely read and loved. But you will find the same theme, restated in different words and different metaphors, running throughout the text. I hope some of my thoughts will resonate with you, as they say, and give you some new perspectives on the magical thing called Story.

TOM SIMON
Calgary
June 2016

STYLE IS THE ROCKET

In certain genres (romance, science fiction and fantasy) formerly relegated to the moribund mass-market paperback, readers care not a whit about cover design or even good writing, and have no attachment at all to the book as object.

—*Steve Wasserman, in The Nation*

DON'T MOCK THE AFFLICTED.' This is a good rule, but it needs a rider: 'Unless they choose to afflict themselves, and treat their affliction as cause for pride.' Colour-blindness is not funny; but a colour-blind man who should proclaim the virtues of his superior eyesight, and sneer at all those who suffer under the illusion that red is different from green, would be the stuff of immortal comedy. He would be laughed at heartily, and have no one to blame for it but himself.

There is a kind of literary colour-blindness which occurs, for the most part, only among highly cultivated people; for such folly in nature is self-correcting. It takes two opposite forms. One is the belief that prose style is all; that a work of literature is only as good as its individual sentences, and that a bland or pedestrian prose style is in itself sufficient to condemn a story as subliterary dreck. The second form I shall discuss later..

This belief is lamentably common among those who profess to teach English or American literature. In part it is bound up with the habit of 'close reading', and with the tenets of New Criticism which hold it improper to judge a story even partly by its dramatic or emotional effect. On these terms, one could not possibly account for the fact that a book can be translated into a film, or even a French book into English; that there is something quite separate from the specific details of the writer's language, which makes the translation recognizably the same story as the original, though there may not be a single word in common between them. But that is a discussion for another time.

For now I want to talk about this: There are whole shoals of critics who judge literature only by its most obvious and meretricious characteristics – the mere details of word choice and sentence-level prose. B. R. Myers, in his excellent critical essay, *A Reader's Manifesto*, derided such critics as 'the sentence cult', and largely blamed them for the decline in the quality of American literary fiction. Unfortunately, he spent most of his manifesto baiting the bear in his own den – making the sentence cultists look like fools by showing how puerile and badly written were the very passages they exalted in the reviews as the acme of 'fine writing'. Laura Miller, in a piece for *Salon* called 'Sentenced to death', points out this weakness in Myers' case:

> Much of "A Reader's Manifesto" is wasted on meticulous analysis of prose style – a choice that does seem at odds with Myers' withering disdain for the sentence cult – when the truth is that you don't need an excellent style to write a great novel. Any critic who begins an essay with the example of Theodore Dreiser's *Sister Carrie* ought to know that. Dreiser wrote clunky, awkward, tone-deaf prose. His novels are notoriously hard to "get into," but I still remember where I was and how I felt as I came to the conclusion of *An American Tragedy*, transfixed by the claustrophobic horror of Clyde Griffith's impending execution. On the level of sentences (or paragraphs, for that matter), DeLillo can write circles around Dreiser, but when it comes to writing novels, Dreiser wipes the floor with the author of *Underworld*.

In fact, Myers and Miller don't appear to disagree about much; they are simply talking past one another. The very fact that Myers praises *Sister Carrie* (with a semi-ironic nod to *Carrie* as well) reveals him as a man who knows that a story is not merely the sum of its sentences. The fact that Miller finds some of Myers' bad examples as ghastly as he does shows that she, too, considers the 'sentence cultists' largely to have failed even on their own terms. In the book-length version of *A Reader's Manifesto,* Myers fires back at Miller with dudgeon. The effect of all this cross-talk is rather comical: as if a mixed Belgian couple should get into a heated argument about a day trip, because he wanted to go to Louvain and she wanted to go to Leuven.

What Myers and Miller would agree on, and the sentence cultists would never understand, is that prose style is only technique, and technique alone does not make a novel. Alas, critics like Steve Wasserman have been with us for at least a century; they seemed to breed like maggots in the *art pour l'art* atmosphere of the 1920s. Thus George Orwell in 'Inside the Whale':

> In 'cultured' circles art-for-art's-saking extended practically to a worship of the meaningless. Literature was supposed to consist solely in the manipulation of words. To judge a book by its subject matter was the unforgivable sin, and even to be aware of its subject matter was looked on as a lapse of taste. About 1928, in one of the three genuinely funny jokes that *Punch* has produced since the Great War, an intolerable youth is pictured informing his aunt that he intends to 'write'. 'And what are you going to write about, dear?' asks the aunt. 'My dear aunt,' says the youth crushingly, 'one doesn't write *about* anything, one just *writes.*'

The trouble is that if one 'just *writes*', one will very soon find that nobody 'just *reads*'. Readers are horribly utilitarian animals; they like value for money, and insist upon value for time, and they like to read *about* something. They flee from people like the intolerable youth in *Punch*; they prefer the fuddy-duddy attitude of the sixteenth century, when it was a truism that writers 'ought to please and instruct'. At the very least writers ought to please *or* instruct, and not merely amuse themselves at the expense of the reading public. No doubt this is a philistine attitude; then again, the whole Western literary tradition was more or less invented by the Greeks, and the Philistines, it now appears, were probably Greeks themselves. I am afraid the intolerable youths just can't win.

It is the very *aboutness* of stories, the fact that the sentences exist only to point to something other and outer and not entirely expressible in words, that enraptures the reader and confounds the critic. *Aboutness* is a very Aristotelian notion: it is what the Philosopher called a 'final cause'. Stories don't exist because a pen made certain marks upon a paper, or because somebody's fingers struck the computer keys in a certain order. They exist because somebody had the *intention* of telling them; and that intention usually involves the desire to help other people see some aspect of the world from one's own perspective. This can be as weighty as Solzhenitsyn's wish to excite pity and revulsion for the horrors of the Gulag; or as light as Chesterton's wish to show people how wonderful it was that the South of England, among many other things, was also a piece of chalk.

But *aboutness*, indeed the whole idea of final causes, is banished from the intellectual toolkit of modern science, which concerns itself solely with what Aristotle called *efficient* causes. From that perspective it is quite true to say that a story exists because the author's fingers struck the keys with so many newtons of force in such and such an order. True, but trivial; factual, but meaningless. It is a very precise answer to the wrong question, because by excluding final causes from its field of inquiry, modern science has put itself in the position of the tech support people in the old joke:

> A helicopter was flying around above Seattle when an electrical malfunction disabled all of the aircraft's electronic navigation and communications equipment. Due to the clouds and haze, the pilot could not determine the helicopter's position

and course to fly to the airport. The pilot saw a tall building, flew toward it, circled, drew a handwritten sign, and held it up in the window. The sign said 'WHERE AM I?' in large letters. People in the tall building drew a sign of their own and held it in one of their own windows. Their sign read: 'YOU ARE IN A HELICOPTER.'

The pilot smiled, waved, set a course for SEATAC airport, and landed safely. After they were on the ground, the co-pilot asked the pilot how he determined their position. The pilot responded: 'I knew that had to be the Microsoft tech support building in Redmond. The response they gave me was technically correct, but completely useless.'

It is technically correct that a story is *expressed* as a series of sentences; but that is completely useless as an explanation of what a story *is*. However, it excludes final causes from consideration, and focuses exclusively on things that can in principle be objectively measured; and to that extent it makes literary criticism look like a scientific activity, deserving of some measure or echo of the prestige that attends the sciences. It is no accident that the New Criticism caught on in the early years of the Cold War, when a massive increase in government grants to the sciences made that section of academia not only more prestigious, but richer and more powerful, than it had ever been before. All through the arts and humanities, one could find professors reacting understandably, if inappropriately, by trying to redefine their disciplines as branches of science. 'Close reading' was a manifestation of this trend. It is what you get when you ignore everything about literature except what can be seen under a microscope.

The microscope reveals just that aspect of literature that I called 'obvious and meretricious' before: prose technique at the sentence level. It is no accident, I think, that the pseudo-scientists of the modern humanities are especially apt to perceive only the obvious and meretricious qualities of other things as well.

A generation ago, there was a lot of cant about the supposed Freudian properties of nuclear missiles. According to this line, male politicians and generals were obsessed with building more and yet more missiles, not because of their military utility or destructive power, but merely because they were shaped like giant phalluses. The entire course of the Cold War was thus explained away as an exercise in competitive penis-envy. I actually knew people who believed this, or at least pretended to. In the deep paranoiac funk of the anti-Reaganite Left of the 1980s, this nonsense practically amounted to received wisdom.

In reality, of course, missiles are not designed to look like phalluses; they are designed to look like arrows, and for the same reason – to make them fly efficiently in a ballistic trajectory. Human beings have been making practical experiments in the art of aerodynamic design for hundreds of thousands of years, since the invention of the throwing spear; they have concerned themselves with *propulsion* systems for airborne projectiles for at least 15,000 years, since the invention of the bow and arrow. If there were a more effective shape for arrows and spears, you may be sure the human race would have invented it. Shields and helmets, cannonballs and land mines, look nothing like penises, but that did not retard their adoption in the slightest.

The real concern of the Cold Warriors was not with the rockets themselves, but with the payload. The rocket was simply the most convenient device for carrying a payload a long way at high speed. It might be built to deliver an H-bomb to Moscow, or Neil Armstrong to the Moon; it was never built just for the sake of having a giant aluminium phallus. Yet it was fashionable in some circles to pretend that it was the rocket, and the *shape* of the rocket, that mattered, and not the cargo that it carried. The parallel with the fallacy of New Criticism and 'close reading' is curiously exact; and the two errors were made, to a considerable extent, by the same people. Professors of English Literature, and other academics of that sort, were exceptionally likely to be Leftist in their political views, and Leftist in a particularly superficial and impractical way. Academic Leftism tends to be far more about expressing the correct opinions and denouncing the correct enemies than about any kind of real political activity.

We can see the same tendency increasingly at work among academics, and to a lesser extent artists, ever since about the middle of the nineteenth century. It was not always so. John Constable was the leading landscape painter of the late Georgian period, but he was also a mill owner's son, and had worked in some of the very mills that he liked to portray in his paintings; indeed, one appreciative critic, looking at a mill in a Constable landscape, said: 'I can see that it will go *round.*' Indeed the most striking feature of English culture at that time is the easy fusion and fluent communication of mechanics with aesthetes, inventors with artists. Nearly all the leading scientific and technical men of the era were expert draughtsmen, and nearly all the great painters of the English school took an abiding interest in natural science and technology, in how things actually worked. That attitude began to disappear in the Victorian period, as art and technology each increased in complexity until an artist or an engineer had to give all his attention to his own field in order to remain *au courant.* Dickens, for all his skill at portraying character, was hopeless at portraying *work.* Here is George Orwell again, in 'Inside the Whale':

> Wonderfully as he can describe an *appearance,* Dickens does not often describe a *process.* The vivid pictures that he succeeds in leaving in one's memory are nearly always the pictures of things seen in leisure moments, in the coffee-rooms of country inns or through the windows of a stage-coach; the kind of things he notices are inn-signs, brass door-knockers, painted jugs, the interiors of shops and private houses, clothes, faces and, above all, food. Everything is seen from the consumer-angle. When he writes about Cokestown he manages to evoke, in just a few paragraphs, the atmosphere of a Lancashire town as a slightly disgusted southern visitor would see it. 'It had a black canal in it, and a river that ran purple with evil-smelling dye, and vast piles of buildings full of windows where there

was a rattling and a trembling all day long, where the piston of the steam-engine worked monotonously up and down, like the head of an elephant in a state of melancholy madness.'...

Nothing is queerer than the vagueness with which he speaks of Doyce's 'invention' in *Little Dorrit*. It is represented as something extremely ingenious and revolutionary, 'of great importance to his country and his fellow-creatures', and it is also an important minor link in the book; yet we are never told what the 'invention' is! On the other hand, Doyce's physical appearance is hit off with the typical Dickens touch; he has a peculiar way of moving his thumb, a way characteristic of engineers. After that, Doyce is firmly anchored in one's memory; but, as usual, Dickens has done it by fastening on something external.

Fastening on something external: I think it can be said, without much exaggeration, that this is the characteristic vice of the modern academic, often of the modern writer and artist, and above all, of the modern critic. The mere *shape* of a rocket, divorced from its function, is an external; the bomb or astronaut on board is the unseen essential. The pistons moving like the heads of elephants were external; what those steam engines were *doing* is essential. In a work of fiction, the details of prose style, viewed sentence by sentence, are external; what is essential is the *experience* of being immersed in the story.

For the plain truth is that reading for pleasure involves putting oneself in a mild trance state, in which the attention is not focused on the words of the story, but on the scenes and images that the story awakens in the reader's imagination. It will do here to remember Samuel Alexander's distinction between what he called *contemplation* and *enjoyment;* or, as I prefer to express it, between the external act of paying *attention* to a process, and the internal act of *performing* it. When you look at the Moon through a telescope, you are *attending* to the Moon and *performing* astronomy. If you go away from the telescope and read Newton's *Principia*, you are now *attending* to astronomy and *performing* the act of reading. And when you read a story, you are at most *attending* to the text on the page, and that in a superficial way; what you are *performing* is the complex business of recreating the events imaginatively, and then the fullest part of your attention is on the scene playing in your head.

Here again we are involved in the dangerous and unscientific business of final causes. Wherever this distinction between attention and performance occurs, we find that the *attention* is on the *efficient* cause of the experience, and the *performance* is the *final* cause. Viewing and comprehending the words on the page is *how* we read, the efficient cause; experiencing the events in our head is *why* we read, the final cause. Any account that eliminates the final cause from consideration, as the New Criticism does, is leaving out half of the process, and without it the other half is unintelligible.

In just the same way, the rocket is *how* the astronaut gets to the Moon or the bomb gets to Russia; but the action of the bomb or astronaut is *why* one takes the trouble to build and launch the rocket. The general with his ICBM is attending to rocketry, but performing nuclear warfare; the people at NASA are also attending to rocketry, but performing the exploration of space. *Why* is more important than *how*.

As we see when the French novel is translated into English, or the English novel into a film, the *why* can survive intact even when the *how* is changed beyond recognition. And as we see with the rocket, the *why* may be drastically different even when the *how* remains exactly the same. Chimpanzees and humans both have hands, but only one of the two species uses its hands to write stories or to play the piano. It is not the opposable thumb that makes the real difference. One can easily type without using the thumbs at all; and the different orientation of the thumb compared to the other fingers is an active nuisance in playing the piano – a considerable amount of technique is devoted to overcoming it. Early piano players did not even use all ten fingers; they played with the middle three fingers of each hand, deeming the thumb and little finger useless. It was only in the time of Berlioz or thereabouts that composers began deliberately writing pieces for the piano that required every digit.

Now, if you are concerned solely with the obvious and meretricious, with *attention* to the exclusion of *performance,* with the *how* and not with the *why*, you will never understand the innumerable variations that appear in the *how.* If you believe that rockets exist solely for the sake of a Freudian demonstration, you will never understand why a Saturn V is bigger than a Minuteman. Your theory will compel you to suppose that the builder of the Saturn V had a worse case of penis envy, or that Strategic Forces generals have less testosterone than NASA administrators. To explain the difference, you have to know the *why.* The Saturn V is bigger because it has a harder job to do: it has to carry a capsule and three astronauts into Earth orbit, which requires much more energy than to deliver a bomb on a ballistic trajectory within the atmosphere. If Cold War generals had really been concerned with showing off the size of their penis-substitutes, they would have mounted their nuclear warheads on Saturn Vs. In reality they did no such thing.

We return now to the 'sentence cult', and to persons like Mr. Wasserman, with his sneering contempt for genre fiction. Mr. Wasserman used to be the book-review editor for the Los Angeles *Times.* As it happens, I know something about the kind of books that used to be favoured by that newspaper. Its editorial policy was to disdain genre fiction, loosely definable as anything with a strong focus on plot, and extol literary fiction, in which the emphasis was all on technique. As B. R. Myers said, 'literary' reviewers could sometimes forgive a strong and compelling plot as long as the prose style called sufficient attention to itself.

But there was a school of critics that disparaged plot altogether, that decried 'formed stories' of any kind, and plumped for sheer stylistic experimentation as the sole acceptable *raison d'être* of fiction. If they had existed as a little claque of their own, they would have been entirely unimportant; but they were determined to impose their views on the world, or at least on the *literati.* This they did by acting rather like 'blocking troops' in the Red Army during the Second World War. They kept the front-line troops steadily advancing by shooting at them from behind. Anyone who did not participate in the assault with sufficient vigour to please them was, according to their lights, a deserter and a traitor to the cause.

It was the influence of this extreme school that secured James Joyce's extravagantly exalted place in the modern literary pantheon. Orwell makes a character in one of his novels opine that 'Lawrence was all right, and Joyce even better before he went off his coconut'. The stylistic extremists would have said that Joyce was better *because* he went off his coconut. They were the ones who mildly disparaged *Dubliners* for its alleged conventionality, and praised the sheer Dada of *Finnegans Wake*. The lack of incident in *Ulysses*, the deliberate dulness of the characters, the sheer impossibility of figuring out what makes this a *story* (unless you recognize the obscure allusions to *The Odyssey* and can tell exactly how and from what Joyce is taking the piss) – these are important flaws, to anyone but a stylistic extremist. But the extremists did their best to shout down anybody who dared to object to these things; instead they piqued themselves on valuing Joyce *because* he was obscure and plotless. ('Even to be aware of its subject matter was looked on as a lapse of taste.') The important thing was to be as 'experimental' as possible; only a philistine would ask whether the experiment succeeded or failed. 'My dear aunt, one doesn't write *about* anything, one just *writes*.'

In fact, the most successful experimental writer of the 1920s and thereabouts is not even recognized as experimental anymore, because his experiments succeeded too well. That was Ernest Hemingway. The essence of his genius was to apply 'telegraphese', the compressed and allusive language of the transatlantic cable reporters, to the short story and the novel. Look at any of Hemingway's novels side by side with his contemporaries, such as Fitzgerald, Woolf, or Joyce himself, and then with a randomly chosen bestseller from any later period up to the 1980s or thereabouts. You will probably find that Hemingway's language resembles the latter-day bestseller much more than it resembles any of his contemporaries. They were still writing the self-consciously 'bookish' language of the Victorian novel, allowing of course for the changes of dialect over time. Hemingway wrote a compact and elliptical language that showed more than it told, and hinted at more than it showed, and derived its patterns of grammar and diction from spoken rather than written English. Few later authors could equal the pith and force of Hemingway's style, but they imitated it as well as they could, until it became the default 'transparent' style for even garden-variety commercial fiction. Heinlein's enormous reputation as a science fiction writer rests partly on his being the first to successfully apply the Hemingway technique to SF.

Paradoxically, the successful experiments of Hemingway are less esteemed by the extremists than the failed experiments of Joyce. *Ulysses* is still exotic after almost a century, because its style is so peculiar, and its structure so opaque, that few writers have tried to imitate it. But nearly everyone imitates Hemingway, usually at several removes, and often without even knowing it. His style is too familiar to *feel* experimental any longer; but a pastiche of Joyce or Gertrude Stein is weird enough to seem fresh, and has the added advantage that most readers will dislike it on sight. Half the business of an extremist is to make sure that the mainstream never catches up with him, and the easiest way to do that is to occupy an extreme that is nowhere near the current. The backwaters of 1920s-style Dada are a perfect breeding-place for this kind of snobbery.

This mania for stylistic weirdness, enforced by the blocking troops of Modernist criticism, led in the end to a situation where even quite ordinary newspaper reviewers would shout praise for the 'experimental' brilliance of bad prose rather than admit to the nudity of the reigning monarch. One of the reigning monarchs of the nineties was Annie Proulx, who was extravagantly lauded for the following sentence in *Accordion Crimes*. A woman has just had her arms chopped off by sheet metal, and this is how Proulx describes it:

> She stood there, amazed, rooted, seeing the grain of the wood of the barn clapboards, paint jawed away by sleet and driven sand, the unconcerned swallows darting and reappearing with insects clasped in their beaks looking like mustaches, the wind-ripped sky, the blank windows of the house, the old glass casting blue swirled reflections at her, the fountains of blood leaping from her stumped arms, even, in the

first moment, hearing the wet thuds of her forearms against the barn and the bright sound of the metal striking.

Every story is a conversation between writer and reader, even though the writer is effectively deaf and seldom hears what the reader is saying. Here is a rough transcript of the conversation as it transpires in the passage above:—

Proulx. My character is stunned. Absolutely gobsmacked. Don't I do a wonderful job of telling you how gobsmacked she is? She's not just amazed, she's *rooted.*

Reader. I don't think that's how people react to having their arms chopped off.

P. Now if I were one of these hack commercial writers, I'd talk about *her.* But see how cleverly I do everything by indirection! See how poetic I am! The barn is built of clapboards, you see—

R. I don't care about the clapboards. This woman is bleeding to death!

P. And you can see the wood grain because the paint has all been worn off, but I wouldn't put it *that* way, oh no, I'm a *Writer,* I am. So I said to myself, what's a better action verb to use in this place? Why, *chewed,* of course! But that's not poetic enough for me, because I'm a Special Snowflake, I am. So I changed it to *jawed* instead. Isn't that original? Aren't I clever? *Look at meeee!*

R. I don't think that word means what you think it means. It doesn't mean *chew;* it means to natter on endlessly, just like you're doing now. Now will you stifle it and get on with the story?

P. Now I describe the swallows, and they're so *ironic,* because they're *unconcerned,* don't you see? And they're just carrying on about their business, darting out of sight and coming back—

R. All this while that poor woman's arms are flying through the air? They must be miles away by now.

P. That's not my point. My *point* is that they're catching *insects,* don't you see, and the insects are like *moustaches!* Isn't that clever? Only a Writer could have come up with that simile! *Look at meee!!*

R. I think you're mistaking me for someone who cares.

P. And then I describe the rest of the scene, and I'm just as clever about that, and the windows don't just make reflections, they make *swirled blue* reflections, because I'm a Writer, I am, and look at me being all impressionist!

R. I think I'm going to skip on a bit.

P. Spoilsport! All right, I'll get in a bit about my character, since you seem so anxious for me to be all boring and nasty and *commercial* and stick to the silly old point. What do you think I am, the six o'clock news? So her blood is spurting, no, that's too ordinary, *leaping* from her stumped arms—

R. You mean from the stumps of her arms. 'Stumped' means something completely different. It has to do with not having a clue, *hint, hint.*

P. I'm a *Writer*, I am, and you can tell because I don't let myself be limited by your silly old bourgeois rules. Her stumped arms, I said, and I'm sticking to it. And then she hears the wet thuds of her forearms—

R. Ewwww.

P. —against the barn, and then the sheet metal hits, and it's not just the sound of it hitting, it's the *bright* sound, because only a Writer would use something as nifty as synaesthesia to put her point across. See? I know about synaesthesia! I'm smart! Look at me! LOOK AT *MEEEEEE!!!!*

R. If you don't get on with the story, I'm going to say the Eight Deadly Words.

P. (momentarily taken aback) Which are?

R. **'I don't care what happens to these people.'** I mean, if you're going to stand there jawing (see, I used the word correctly) about swallows and moustaches and swirly blue windows, while the woman you have just mutilated is bleeding her life away – well, if *you* care as little as *that* about your own characters, I don't see why *I* should give a damn. You haven't even noticed that she's in *pain!*

P. (angrily) This isn't *about* her. This is about me! Me, *meee*, wonderful **ME!!** Damn you, *why aren't you looking at **ME!!!***

Of course this conversation is ruthlessly suppressed in the New York *Times* review by Walter Kendrick, who singled out that very sentence, in all its scarlet and purple excess, as 'brilliant prose'. B. R. Myers was kinder to Proulx, if only in the interest of brevity:

> The last thing Proulx wants is for you to start wondering whether someone with blood spurting from severed arms is going to stand rooted long enough to see more than one bird disappear, catch an insect, and reappear, or whether the whole scene is not in bad taste of the juvenile variety.

The sad truth, I am afraid, is that self-consciously 'literary' writers do not write to be *read*; they write to impress the critics, and if their ambitions are particularly lofty, to have their books made required reading for hapless English majors. Then the English majors, or a depressingly large percentage of them, buy into the pernicious notion that this self-regarding drivel really *is* 'brilliant prose' – and, still more, that brilliancy of prose is the primary and sufficient *purpose* of literature – and the whole sorry swindle is perpetuated for another generation.

Proulx's star has more or less fallen since Myers launched his attack, but the sentence cult goes on. Wasserman appears to be a card-carrying member. When he says that genre readers 'care not a whit about good writing', what he really means is that they are not apt to be bamboozled by pinchbeck pyrotechnics and stylistic bull. And God bless them for it – say the rest of us.

There is, of course, another side to the story. If style is the rocket that propels the payload of fiction, it must be adequate to the task. It would be unspeakably stupid to build a Saturn V merely as a phallic totem; but there is an opposite fault, which is to attach the payload to a rocket too small to lift it off the ground at all. Then the astronaut goes nowhere, or the H-bomb— Well, 'tis the sport to have the enginer hoist with his own petard; but not if the petard hoists the audience and the whole neighbourhood along with him.

The patron saint of inadequate prose is still probably Isaac Asimov, who once frankly admitted, 'All I expect of my prose is to be clear.' Clarity is greatly to be admired, and in many kinds of nonfiction it is enough. It is a pity that Asimov was not interested in computers; then we might have had some decent software manuals instead of the slush-by-committee that we usually get. But in fiction it is *not* enough to 'tell it like it is'. As Ursula Le Guin pointed out in 'From Elfland to Poughkeepsie', in story the language has to carry the whole load: 'there is no *is* without it'.

Asimov was fond of the analogy of plate glass and stained glass. A stained-glass window may be a great work of art, he said, but it does not allow you to see what is going on in the street. For that you want plate glass, absolutely clear and unadorned – just as Asimov's prose is clear and unadorned. But this is specious. In fiction, *there is no street.* What we want instead is a window that produces the *illusion* of the street. The glass needs to be tinted and patterned so finely, so cunningly, that we are half convinced that we are looking *through* it when we are only looking *at* it.

Stephen R. Donaldson expressed the metaphor perfectly when he made it the central conceit of *Mordant's Need.* Magic in that novel is done by Imagers, who make mirrors with just that magical quality; and if the illusion is done well enough, it becomes *real,* and the Imager can reach through the glass and pull objects out of the place that the mirror reveals. (A klutz of an apprentice Imager accidentally uses such a mirror to pull the story's heroine out of her apartment in midtown Manhattan. Of all the ways that earthly mortals have been translated into fantasy worlds, this is surely among the most interesting.)

If I may be permitted the metaphor, Hemingway was an Imager; he almost invented the art. His apparently plain and journalistic style was wonderfully deceptive: it communicated more by tone and implication than the average Victorian novelist could communicate by blatant rhetoric. Not only that, he mastered the difficult art of making the picture look as if it extended beyond the window frame in all directions, so that the reader would guess at the outlines of the larger scene and be moved by them. He first demonstrated this technique in 'A Clean, Well-Lighted Place', from which he deliberately amputated the beginning and ending, and carefully inserted just such cues in the middle as would let the reader infer what had been removed.

Asimov's stories tend to have the opposite effect. By striving for a naturalistic 'plate glass' prose style, he makes his stories look like stage-pieces, and not very well-staged ones at that. The effect is worst in the novels he wrote in the 1980s, when he took up writing science fiction on a large scale after twenty-five years away from the field. His Robot novels and his Foundation series, each taken separately, have this much of the Hemingway quality, that they do convincingly seem to extend in all directions beyond the limits of the text. But when he decided to combine the two series, he spoilt the effect. Instead of weaving them together into a larger whole, he made them *smaller*. The whole was less than the sum of its parts; the whole was less than some of the individual parts. The crucial error was to make R. Daneel Olivaw the unseen prime mover of the Foundation stories. The original tales were about millions of worlds and quadrillions of people working out their destiny against an infinite background of space and time. The post-Daneel books were about a handful of carefully crafted puppets pretending to be human while the all-powerful robot pulled everyone's strings. *Every* mystery had the same answer: Daneel dunnit!

If Asimov had been a better prose stylist – if his rocket had been able to propel that unwieldy payload – then the excitement of the journey might have obscured the triviality of the destination. E. E. 'Doc' Smith was not a master of prose, but he was good enough for his own purpose: his rocket would fly. He had a genuine gift for expressing sublimity. Smith can make you *feel* the immensity of space, the smallness of Man, and the colossal powers that living things must summon up to make an imprint on the vastness of the universe. There are many things he does *not* make you feel, but those are not the things his stories are about. We do not expect a rocket to double as a submarine. Asimov's trouble is his relentless claustrophilia: he flinches as if by reflex from the sublime, and even from the merely big. His most characteristic scenes are set in offices and laboratories, classrooms and auditoriums, or in the staterooms and command decks of featureless spaceships. One of his stories, 'Thiotimoline to the Stars', is entirely about a lecture delivered in an auditorium – which, we find out only at the end, has travelled from Earth to Saturn and back again while the lecturer was talking.

It is almost as if Asimov's brain had no budget for special effects. His powers of description were so limited that his rocket could not lift any substantial payload off the ground. The *idea* behind the combined Robot-and-Foundation universe (until R. Daneel became a *deus ex machina*) could have produced stories of cathartic intensity and mind-boggling scope: the sort of stories that Asimov himself described as 'novas'. But that would have required a better writer than Asimov allowed himself to be. The payload was a team of explorers fit to explore a galaxy, but the rocket never budged beyond the confines of the small indoor set where the story was obviously staged.

In the film *A Hard Day's Night*, Wilfrid Brambell (playing Paul McCartney's fictitious grandfather) complains: 'Lookit, I thought I was supposed to be getting a change of scenery. And so far I've been in a train and a room, and a car and a room, and a room and a room.' He could have been complaining about the view of the universe from an Asimov story.

It ought to be mere common sense that the rocket should be made big enough to carry the payload. But among writers and still more among critics, such common sense seems hard to come by. On one hand we have the aesthetes, the people who think the style *is* the novel, the medium *is* the message, and that the rocket (divested of its payload) exists only to serve as a gigantic surrogate penis. On the other hand we have the 'plate glass' people, who think that the payload is everything, that the *plot* is the novel, or the idea is the story, and that if you come up with a strong enough concept, it will fly of its own accord. But books do not write themselves, and astronauts do not reach the Moon by waving their arms or even by wishing their hardest. *How* to construct a rocket to lift a given payload is a matter of complex engineering; and how to construct a text to carry a given story is a matter of difficult skill. I shall not pretend to explain such matters here. But unless we can get away from our fixations on style-as-all or idea-as-all, the flights of fantasy that we call stories will be unrewarding, and our voyages will be unmercifully short.

THE DRUDGE AND THE ARCHITECT

S OME HOURS AGO the idea of this *essai* came to me, hard and clear, demanding to be written, and proposing for itself the title, 'Hard Work *vs.* Working Hard'. 'Always,' said Kipling, 'in our trade, look a gift horse at both ends and in the middle. He may throw you': therefore I did a quick search, and found another essay with that exact title, by one Scott McGrath. What he has to say is good, and valid, and useful, and I propose to take it as a starting-point; but his essay is general in application, and I want to apply the distinction particularly to the business of writing. So I have changed my title to 'The Drudge and the Architect', for reasons I mean to make clear later..

Here is the nub or gist of Mr. McGrath's piece:

> Working hard doesn't mean you're doing hard work. It doesn't even mean you're doing good or smart work. It just means you're expending a lot of energy and a lot of time towards the completion of some task....
>
> So what is hard work and how do you know if you're doing it?
>
> ... For me, knowing I'm doing or about to do hard work doesn't get signaled in the brain. It's in the kishkes – that part of your stomach that you don't know exists until some thing

is really bothering you. When your kishkes start turning, you know you're onto something important.... Our kishkes are also pretty good at preventing us from doing the hard work we need to do, if we let them.

For my own purposes, I shall define 'hard work' and 'working hard' by means of examples; and since I am a conservative stick-in-the-mud of antediluvian origin, I shall humour myself by choosing examples that were fresh in the world when I was comparatively young.

By 'working hard', I mean doing a demanding task until you are tired and cannot do it anymore. Digging ditches for twelve hours by brute muscle power is working hard. It does not even matter to my definition whether you use a shovel; though it matters very much for other purposes, such as getting the ditch dug. But if all you do is bend your back and exert yourself until you have to rest, you have been working hard – even if you have nothing to show for it at the end of the day. A mouse could dig a ditch by working hard, but it would have to be a very long-lived mouse.

By 'hard work', I mean a task that cannot be accomplished by any amount of exertion or back-bending, unless aided by skill and invention. Building the Pyramids was hard work. Those limestone blocks weigh (as I was told by a foreman on the worksite, when I went round to see what all the noise was about) some two tons apiece. You could bend your back and exert yourself until the Nile ran dry, and not move one of those blocks an inch. The mouse that could dig a ditch could not even make a start on a Pyramid.

Fortunately, my old friend Imhotep (I speak imprecisely; I admired the man, but he never returned my calls) was a shrewd chap, and knew how to bridge the gap between working hard and hard work. First, he did not employ mice to build his pyramid. Second, he used pulleys and levers, and ramps and rollers, and water to reduce friction, and other such things as would give his workmen a mechanical advantage and make their hard working *go*. Nowadays we have improved upon these methods. We have bulldozers and cranes, backhoes and trucks, and all kinds of machines not limited by the power of human muscles; so that we can do many kinds of hard work without working hard at all. It was fashionable, during the 'ancient astronauts' craze of the seventies, to claim that modern industrial man could not possibly duplicate the Pyramids. This is false. In fact there is already a project afoot to build an exact duplicate of the Great Pyramid of Khufu in Washington, D.C.; construction to commence in thirty or forty years' time, once the environmental impact study is done.

Mutatis mutandis, our minds can work hard, and they can do hard work, but there is no necessary connection between the two. The stereotype of 'working hard' in the Information Age is Suzie Cobol, the 'code grinder' who just barely squeezed through her computer science degree and spends her days laboriously tracking down bugs in reams and reams of other people's code. (Sometimes called 'Sammy Cobol' in an attempt to avoid the appearance of sexism; but let's face it, the hackers who use these terms scarcely regard COBOL programmers as human at all, regardless of sex.) The pinnacle of 'hard work' is the programming genius who invents a nifty new algorithm, replacing an enormous amount of brute-force calculation with about twenty lines of efficient code. Indeed, the invention of the computer itself was hard work, and it did away with a lot of working hard: ENIAC, the first Turing-complete electronic computer, was built to calculate artillery firing tables, a job previously done by sheer intellectual drudgery.

I am not a programming genius any more than I am Imhotep, but these and other cases have filled me with a lifelong respect for those who do hard work, and a sort of comparative pity for those who can only work hard. For convenience I shall call the first kind Architects, and the second kind Drudges, and capitalize the names to signalize the fact that I am using the words as terms of art and not in the usual way.

Now, this is not the same distinction as that, popular among time-management gurus, between 'working hard' and 'working smart'. It is not the difference between two working methods, but the difference between a method of working and a kind of work to be done. Drudges can 'work smart', and often do; and their reward is that instead of exhausting themselves at their jobs, they can knock off at the end of the day with enough energy left for their families and their amusements.

Frank Gilbreth, the pioneering efficiency expert, used to look for the laziest man on the job, knowing he would be just the one to 'work smart' for the sake of not working hard. But that did not make the lazy man able to do Gilbreth's job, for Gilbreth's job was hard work.

Sometimes 'working smart' means no more than contracting out part of the drudgery to other Drudges: as in the case of the woman who was working on a Ph.D. in Ancient Greek, and spent a year or more gathering and collating her texts, only to find that the whole corpus of Ancient Greek literature had meanwhile been published on a single CD-ROM, the *Thesaurus Linguae Grecae*. Whereupon, instead of mourning and cursing the Fates, she threw away her drudge-work and bought a copy of the disc. What remained to do was the original part of her thesis, which (though I have not read it) I am happy to believe was the work of an Architect.

Now, the particular art or game of writing fiction can be approached in either way: that is, it can be done by a Drudge or by an Architect. I am not here drawing a distinction between bad and good authors. There have been a great many good stories written by Drudges, and some risible flops written by Architects. Still less do I make any claim about the popularity of drudge-work *vs.* architecture. I am not even drawing a distinction between two separate groups of writers. A writer may work as an Architect in his prime, developing new skills and techniques that influence and are copied by generations of writers after him; and then in his senescence he may become a mere Drudge, writing book after book using his own tools and in a pastiche of his own earlier style. Hemingway was almost as famous for becoming a Drudge as for having been an Architect.

Now that I have said what I am *not* doing, let us get on with what I am doing. The Architects, the people doing hard work, are the writers who wrote stories that required them to invent new tools and techniques. Often these are the writers whose books remain most readable after a span of many years. They were being boldly original, which is why the existing techniques were inadequate to the stories they had to tell. Originality is a congenial quality, and boldness is nearly always fun. Certainly a boldly original story is better fun than a story that is derivative and trying timidly to conceal the fact.

Purely for my own interest (for I do not suppose many people will be interested in these ramblings of mine), here is a partial list of Architects who were, so to speak, in my own line of development – those who invented tools that I have tried to acquire for my own little kit.

The grand original, at least among authors we know of by name, is of course Homer, who invented the epic. There were *aoidoi* among the Greeks before him, and the epic hexameter was not a new thing; but he seems to have raised it to a new seriousness of subject-matter and intensity of poetic feeling, never seen before and seldom since equalled. The *Beowulf* poet applied the epic technique to the language and legend of the ancient North, and may have invented the literary device of the 'virtuous pagan' viewed in retrospect from a Christian moral and historical standpoint. The author or compiler of the *Elder Edda* seems to have been the first to combine myth and epic into an organized 'Matter', making explicit the connection between the 'foreground' legends and the 'background' aetiological tales. (*The Silmarillion* could in this light be classified as an edda.)

Shakespeare almost single-handedly fashioned Modern English into a language fit for high imaginative literature, and refocused his borrowed plots on the psychology of the comic or tragic hero. Daniel Defoe introduced the novel to English, and grounded his novels in the dense realistic detail that he had learnt to write as a pioneering journalist. Sir Walter Scott invented the key techniques of the historical novel, giving his characters the attitudes, and his settings the realia, of the eras in which they were set, instead of representing them in modern dress and with modern habits. Mark Twain cleared away the stylisms of 'bookish' language and told tales in the plain colloquial English of ordinary speech. William Morris contributed the pure 'high' fantasy milieu, what Tolkien later called the 'Secondary World', deliberately unconnected with 'the fields we know'.

Hemingway, a journalist like Defoe, discovered a new literary idiom in the 'telegraphese' of transatlantic cables, by the use of which he put across the bare gist of a story and left the reader to infer the details from minimal clues. Heinlein applied the Hemingway method to science fiction, doing away with the detailed description of wondrous technology and describing it purely by showing its direct role in the actions of the characters. (This was a remarkable invention, by the way. Hemingway left the reader to infer things she might reasonably be expected to know from everyday life. Heinlein trusted her to infer the new and imaginary; indeed, to guess out the technological conceit that underpinned the rest of the story, what Darko Suvin calls the *novum.*) And of course there is Tolkien, whose innovations I have fortunately no need to recapitulate here.

Every one of these Architects left, as the evidence of his contribution to the art of fiction, one or more enduring landmarks of literature, as prominent, and to date as well-preserved, as Imhotep's expertly piled stones. But do not suppose that a writer has to create an utterly new technique to be an Architect. All of us become Architects, in our small way, when we set ourselves to write stories beyond our skill; when we have to learn and master tools that are new to us, though they may be as old as Story itself.

It is then that we cross the line from merely working hard to attempting hard work. It is then that we move from the derivative to the original; from ringing the changes to casting new bells. I am not fond of the term 'hack' as applied to writers, but if it means anything, it means a writer who stays safely within the limits of his own established know-how, rearranging the bricks in his Lego set for a safe pay packet. He may be a Drudge indeed, who works virtuously long hours with his fixed and finished set of tools, but he has shut himself off from the chance of becoming more. He lives and dies by the maxim of Napoleon: 'An army that remains within its fortifications is already beaten.'

A pernicious belief is making the rounds, encouraged by some of the great gurus of self-publishing and self-promotion. The idea is that you have to pay your dues as a writer, by writing some set quantity (some say 500,000 words, some say a million) of inferior prose, after which you will magically become a Commercial Writer, and be able to make a fine living if only you are prolific enough, and never have to learn anything again – at least about writing; you will always have more lessons about marketing to learn from the gurus. It is the Gospel according to Drudge; the fatal promise that you will never have to do hard work – that working hard is enough. But in this game, to stop learning is to repeat yourself, and to repeat yourself is to begin to die.

To write prolifically is a good thing, but it is not the best thing; it is not even the best thing for a writer as such. Be prolific for practice, be prolific to expose your work to more readers, be prolific to try out new techniques and reduce the risk that attends a failure. But for the love of all the Muses, don't be prolific for the mere sake of commercial success; and don't expect that writing ever-larger quantities of the same old stuff will push you over the threshold of commercial success. In the end, quantity is only a multiplier; it is quality that sells. Ten bad stories may sell ten times as much as one bad story; but one good story will outsell a thousand bad ones, and one great story will outlast all the merely good stories you could ever write.

Working hard may earn you a wage, but it will always be a poor one, because anybody can work hard. The real rewards of this game are in doing hard work. The gold is not in the twice-worked tailings, but in the hard rock that has never yet been mined. Fame is not in the twice-told tale, but in the tale that only you can discover how to tell; the tale written in the ink of your heart's blood, for which no chemist can prescribe a substitute.

All writing advice is bad for some writers, and some of it is bad for everyone. But if I had to back *one* bit of advice as good for every writer, it would be this: Reach for the heavens, and stretch yourself till they come within your grasp. Don't just work hard; do the hard work. Be a Drudge if you have to, but strive to be an Architect.

THE IMMERSIVE WRITER

'I have learned two ways to tie my shoes. One way is only good for lying down. The other way is good for walking.'
—*Robert A. Heinlein, Stranger in a Strange Land*

A S EVERYONE KNOWS, there are two ways of doing a thing: one way and the other way. For any given thing worth doing, there may be an infinite number of ways to divide it into two categories; just as you can cut an apple in two at an infinite number of angles. All these lines of division are technically valid, of course, but some are more helpful than others.

There are, accordingly, two ways of reading books; but infinitely many ways to divide up the act of reading into two classes. One way, which I and others have found useful, is to divide reading into the *immersive* and the *analytic*. If you prefer, you can call them 'reading for the story' and 'reading for the text'. The immersive reader dives joyously into the vicarious experience of the story, identifies with the characters, laughs at the funny bits, cries at the moving bits, and generally wallows in the sensuous details of the story-world. The text is translated on the fly into a sort of 3-D movie playing inside the immersive reader's head. Vladimir Nabokov affected to despise the immersive reader. The analytic reader, who is most often found in academia, stays carefully on the surface of the text, studying the language word by word and sentence by sentence, looking for nuggets of technique and jewels of craftsmanship, and treating motifs and symbols as if they were algebraic variables. Nabokov courted and lionized the analytic reader; which is why Nabokov's books are read (now that the naughty-naughty of *Lolita* has been eclipsed by a planet full of Internet porn) chiefly by bored university students labouring their way through the 'close reading' of a set text.

It will appear that my sympathies are altogether with the immersive reader. This is an oversimplification. Immersive reading, like genre writing or comedy acting, requires a lot more skill than meets the eye. Every immersive reader is capable of reading analytically. If you want the proof of this, take an average romance reader (who could fairly stand as the paragon of immersiveness), and put a cookbook or an airport timetable in front of her. She will not immerse herself in the lives and loves of the parsley; she will not have raptures and rhapsodies about the three o'clock flight to LaGuardia. She will read ruthlessly and efficiently for information, staying very definitely on the surface of the text, but keenly on the watch for any sign that the narrative (so to speak) is unreliable. Then, once she has extracted the data she wants, she will turn back to her Nora Roberts or Barbara Cartland and lose herself once more in the sensuous delights of the bare-chested hero and the throbbing heart of the heroine. What she will not do is read analytically for *fun*. That is a specialized taste, and for various reasons, it is a taste cultivated largely by people who have not got the knack of reading immersively.

As a writer of fiction, one can try to appeal either to the immersive or to the analytic reader; seldom or never to both. I have nothing to say about how to appeal to analytic readers: I don't do that kind of writing myself, know very little about how it is done, and frankly, have not much interest in it. But I can say a little about some of the ways of writing so as to appeal to immersive readers.

There are, of course (sticking to our method here), two ways of writing for immersive readers, and we may once again call them the immersive and the analytic. It may sound odd that you can reach immersive readers by analytic writing, but like many odd things, it is true just the same. The technique is not one I tend to use, but I can at least roughly describe it.

The analytic writer has the same relationship to stories that the food chemist has to cookery. He knows which monkey tricks will produce what emotional responses; he knows the formula for his genre – five parts Cops And Robbers, one part Boy Meets Girl, and three parts Travelogue Through Interesting Places, seasoned to taste with sex and Worcestershire sauce; simmer over medium heat until hard-boiled and cynical. (This, if I remember my Mrs. Beeton's, is the recipe for a Thriller Soufflé.) This method of constructing stories was widely popular among writers for the old pulp magazines. To make a living from the pulps, you had to be immensely prolific, and writing to a formula is the easiest way to increase your output. Besides, the pulps' readers were mostly young, inexperienced, and technically undemanding, and would devour reams of third-rate writing without audible complaint; better writing would not exactly have been wasted on them, but it was not worth doing for a penny a word. This analytic method is still the usual technique in run-of-the-mill writing for films and television. It is sometimes called 'the Old Baloney Factory' by its practitioners; critics, a less genial breed, tend to call it hackwork.

The advantage of the analytic method is that it is *reliable:* it leaves little or nothing to inspiration. Writing by this method consists chiefly in the ingenious manipulation of set story elements, mixed together in the prescribed proportions. It is relatively easy to do; if originality fails, the formula will see you through. The disadvantage, of course, is that it is *predictable* – it leaves little or no *room* for inspiration. Once you have seen all the elements of a particular formula half a dozen times, you've seen them all, and the stories lose the power to surprise you; eventually they lose the power to move your emotions in any way.

This, possibly, is one of the reasons why some people give up on immersive reading and turn to analytics instead. Having been swindled once too often, they decide that *all* immersive reading is a swindle, and take all their reading pleasure from the detective game of catching out the swindler. They read in the spirit of the tiresome people who go to a magic show not to be entertained, but only to figure out how the conjuror works his illusions. And like the know-it-all at the magic show, half their tiresomeness comes from their attitude of sniggering superiority to the unwashed masses who actually watch the show to be amused.

The immersive writer, on the other hand, is unreliable and unpredictable. He writes in an approximate reversal of the immersive reader's process: the story plays itself like a movie in his head, and he tries to capture as much as he can in words. He is never satisfied with the result; the waking dream was so much more vivid than anything that survives translation into language and back again. But he persists, and wrestles thanklessly with his material and technique, and once in a while, with luck and skill, catches lightning in a bottle and produces a remarkable and original story.

I do not want to give a misleading impression. Not all immersive writers are eye-minded. Some perceive their stories chiefly in terms of sound; these tend to be heavy on dialogue and short on visual description. Some perceive them in terms of the naked emotions and interactions of the characters; they are, so to speak, possessed by the viewpoint character until his spirit is exorcised through the pen. These writers can be very interesting, because (if skilful) they can generate tremendously powerful emotional effects. What Robert Frost said – 'No tears in the writer, no tears in the reader' – is especially and vividly true for such people.

It will appear, once again, that my sympathies all lie with the immersive writer; and once again, it is not that simple. Nothing makes worse reading than an *inept* immersive writer. In the first place, the movie in the writer's head may be a hotchpotch of recycled tropes, gleaned not from life (that unpredictable and therefore interesting *auteur*) but from too trustful a reading of the canned motifs and stock responses vended by the Old Baloney Factory. This is one reason why fiction by *young* writers is so seldom good reading. Christopher Paolini, in his tender years when he wrote *Eragon,* was not a hack, but the work of his heart, the interior drama of his soul, was largely strung together from bits and pieces of other people's hackwork. The immersive writer needs more time and experience to mature than is commonly true of the analytic.

More to the point, just as every immersive reader necessarily has a certain amount of analytic skill, every immersive writer needs an analytic side to serve as his first editor and internal critic. This analytic side is the annoying voice in every well-adjusted immersive that continually whispers: 'This was fun to write, but will it be fun to read? Does it advance the story? Is it relevant? Does it serve what we're trying to accomplish here, or are we just being self-indulgent?' These questions need to be asked. A really fluent writer will learn to operate with a sort of mental bifurcation: the analytic mind learns how to contribute its meed while the immersive mind is creating, and in such a way that the immersive mind does not start crying and hide in a corner from the cold cruel world. Most writers have to exercise the two faculties alternately – first create in passion, then edit in cold blood.

Then, of course, one must bear in mind that I am oversimplifying – making a false dichotomy out of what is, after all, only one element in a tremendously complex creative process. Sometimes you *need* false dichotomies to make sense of a continuum. Not everything in life is black and white, but if we want to measure a shade of grey, we need black and white as the standards of comparison. When we say that Greenland is further north and Tahiti is further south, we depend implicitly on the North and South Poles to stop where they are, so other places can be located in relation to them. The pure analytic and the pure immersive are rather like the poles: frigid and infertile wastes where nobody actually lives, but terribly handy to the rest of us for giving directions by.

In 1991, John Cleese gave a famous talk on creativity, in which he drew a sharp contrast between what he called the 'open mode' and the 'closed mode'. The open mode is playful, freewheeling, intuitive, but not logical and often not conventionally productive. The closed mode is logical, methodical, critical; it rips through set tasks with ruthless efficiency, but gets rather lost when there is nobody to tell it what to do. Cleese says that all creativity necessarily takes place in the open mode. It would be fair to say that the immersive writer works most of the time in the open mode, and the analytic writer tends more towards the closed mode. Of course every creative artist needs both modes; this is a tendency rather than an absolute division. Cleese himself, by his own account, is an immersive writer. He gives away his position by this remark in the talk:

> I was always intrigued that one of my Monty Python colleagues who seemed to be, to me, more talented than I was, did never produce scripts as original as mine; and I watched for some time, and then I began to see why. If he was faced with a problem, and fairly soon saw a solution, he was inclined to take it; even though, I think, he knew the solution was not very original. Whereas if I was in the same situation, although I was sorely tempted to take the easy way out and finish by five o'clock, I just couldn't. I'd sit there with the problem for another hour and a quarter, and by sticking with it, would in the end almost always come up with something more original.

This is the hallmark of the immersive writer whose analytic mind remains always on duty. The job of Cleese's immersive faculty, working in the 'open mode', was to come up with funny ideas. The job of the analytic side was to evaluate the ideas as they came out, and say – gently, not cruelly – 'That's too easy; I know you can come up with something better,' and send the immersive mind repeatedly back to its work until it came up with something that passed muster. In this process, the analytic mind is not actually operating in the closed mode; instead, it is acting as a kind of valve or gateway between the open and closed modes, making sure that only the choicest products of the open mode are let through for the mind to work on later in the closed mode. The mind in the closed mode is a factory hand, not an artist, and is strictly limited by the quality of the raw materials you give it to work with. Cleese made sure to give only the best to his.

My own working method is somewhat similar; and since it is seldom or never mentioned in the how-to books for writers, it may be worth describing here. I should caution you that I am *not* recommending this method to anyone; I would not use it myself if I had a good alternative, because it requires an extremely high level of concentration, which is easily disrupted by distraction or ill-health, and is too tiring to keep up for more than a few hours a day. In fact, I am not operating on that level right now; I don't generally need it for non-fiction, and particularly not for these informal *essais*, which are more about exploring my own thoughts in writing than trying to edify others. This is why, when I start up the mill after an interval of writer's block, I nearly always warm up by writing a couple of *essais* before I graduate to the more difficult task of composing fiction.

What happens is that I create what Cleese calls a space-time oasis – a set interval of time that I can spend in a place relatively free of distractions. For this purpose I find that an all-night diner works well. The light buzz of the customers and staff and background music actually help my mind focus inward on itself: the very light effort of ignoring these noises tends to improve my concentration. Then, too, if I am interrupted in such a place, it is seldom important and never urgent, and I can deal with it summarily ('Yes, thank you, I'll have another Diet Coke') without breaking my immersive state. Cleese recommends making the oasis last for about an hour and a half; I like to let mine run longer – up to three hours or so – chiefly because, as a solitary man, I have the luxury of doing so. The signal to emerge from the oasis is that my laptop battery is about to run out.

Once in this oasis, and once the babble and kerfuffle of what C. S. Lewis calls 'the voluble self' have subsided, I give my attention to the immersive experience of the current scene in the story I am writing. I start by re-reading the last bit that I have written, to place myself correctly in the story and remind myself of the setting and mood. Once I can picture it clearly, I let the performance begin to play itself out slowly in my mind. Slowly, because I cannot type as fast as my characters can talk; and still more because I use speech-tags and description and 'business' to measure out the dialogue, introducing pauses and caesuras at needful points, so that the characters' talk comes out at a natural-seeming pace instead of being blurted out in solid chunks. The silences and *ums, ers,* and *you-knows* in actual conversation serve the same purpose – to regulate the timing; you might say that I stick in my description of the scene in place of these conversational noises. Often, like John Cleese composing a Python skit, I have to send my characters back to come up with something better to say; something pithier, more emotionally revealing, or more relevant to the scene. It may take several runs through a short bit of dialogue before I get the feel of it right.

As for the 'business', since I am a fantasy writer, I am in the position that most writers nowadays find themselves in, and that fantasy writers have been in all along. That is, I cannot measure out my conversations by making the characters play with tobacco. Thousands of fictional conversations have been meted out to the rhythm of sucking on cigarettes, striking matches, and tapping the dottles out of villainous pipes. None of my characters are addicted to recreational fire-eating, so I have to work harder to give them something to do. Facial expressions and body language come in handy here; physical action is still better. If two characters can have a talk whilst travelling across country, or doing something else physically strenuous and requiring a bit of dexterity, this gives me a ready and original stock of business, and gives them a handy way of showing their emotional states without cheap theatrics.

If, as it often happens, the scene is *not* one involving much (or any) dialogue, I have a similar problem of pacing: how to keep the physical action moving whilst interlarding it with enough static description to keep the reader informed about where things are and what the character's environment is like. One falls into a natural rhythm here, something like making sandwiches: a slice of description, two pieces of action, and another slice of description on top, with a pickle and mustard shoved in between. This creates a template from which I can suddenly depart at any time to convey surprises and other emotional effects. The techniques of dramatic description and action writing have been discussed and dissected by far abler persons than I; I shall not bore you with my versions of them here. I just find that it is helpful to establish this kind of normal mix or *entrelacement* of action and description, or dialogue and business, to give each scene a fairly consistent background colour against which the foreground actions will more clearly contrast.

Now, where my technique begins to differ sharply from most writers is that I tend to juggle all these considerations *in the first draft*. The movie in my head has its scenery and action, its dialogue and business, and I don't need to put them all across; in fact, it is better not to – to mention only the most telling details, and leave the reader's mind to supply the rest, in the interest of keeping the story moving. But if I leave a detail out of the first draft, I generally lose it for ever. Sometimes, indeed, I will so compress an action scene that I *leave out the action itself*, describing only the lead-up and the after-effects; but this is done deliberately and for effect. There is, for instance, this bit from the opening chapter of *The End of Earth and Sky:*

> The stranger made no answer, but brandished his stick like a weapon. There was a flash of light and a loud bang. Bron's grin vanished as he fell backwards in the thicket. Dropping his pack and drawing a broad-bladed dagger, the stranger sprinted across the meadow to pounce on Bron's twitching form. He jerked Bron's head back and slit his throat with one swift stroke. Then he stood up, licked the blood off his blade, and threw his head back in an ear-splitting yell of triumph—
>
> A crossbow-bolt sprouted from his neck like the first crocus of spring. He fell heavily to the ground. Håkar ran at him, screaming with rage, stabbing wildly with his spear. Bright blood fountained from the stranger's chest. My bow dropped from my nerveless fingers, and I was noisily sick in the grass.

It is only afterwards that the narrator notices that his crossbow has been discharged, and puts two and two together and realizes that *he* shot the stranger. In the heat of the moment he acted on intuition or instinct, faster than his conscious awareness could follow; and I defer the realization to the time when his conscious mind caught up, instead of giving a blow-by-blow description in real time.

Now, some writers would have written the blow-by-blow description first, and rearranged the order of the narrative in revision (or not). But my method is almost entirely immersive. I put myself imaginatively in the character's head, drawing on memories of certain fights I had in my younger days (in which, however, nobody was killed or seriously hurt), and played out the whole scene almost exactly as it stands – *including* the delayed realization. That was there from the beginning; I knew by experience that there was no *time* for him to notice trivial details like the fact that his crossbow had happened to shoot its bolt. Still less would he have paid much attention to his own actions. At such moments you are painfully aware of what is happening all around you, but you don't have the close awareness of your own actions, almost pornographic in detail, that writers are liable to impute to their characters when writing from the Old Baloney Factory.

I give this example in some detail, because it is so very unlike the method usually prescribed by how-to-write books, and especially by gurus of the 'all writing is rewriting' school. It is, in fact, true that this whole scene was done as a revision: once I had done a draft of the story, I saw that the main conflict was not introduced early enough, and devised poor Bron's death as a way to bring it forward into the opening chapter. But the scene itself, once written, was hardly revised at all. I cut it a little, and added one or two details that I wanted for other purposes later in the book, but which would be easier to take in if I introduced them at that earlier stage. Sometimes all the revision I do to a scene is to stick in an explanatory sentence, so as to save myself a paragraph of tedious exposition somewhere else in the story.

In a similar vein, I have been known to hold up in mid-sentence for fifteen minutes whilst sending the immersive mind back, over and over, to come up with a better bit of business than yet another facial expression or tone of voice. I *know* what the characters felt at that point in the scene; but how did they *reveal* it? What, as a poker player would say, were their 'tells'? Many writers would be content to put down something pat and obvious at that stage, or leave it out entirely, and go back and fix it in revision. But I find that if I do not get all the emotional 'beats' right the first time, the action will not go; the immersive mind becomes lazy and sloppy, and relies on the analytic mind to come up with second-hand ideas to fill out the sketchy scene – the Baloney Factory again. So, like John Cleese staying long after quitting time until he came up with an original idea, I brood over a single detail until I get it exactly right. That detail, for all I know, could be the key to the character or to the scene. It often is.

Or I will hang fire over a verb – verbs are the trouble in writing; verbs are the killers; there are never enough vivid verbs, even in English, which is why people have such need of adverbs – because I see a bit of action happening in my mind's eye, I know exactly what it *looks* like, but the scene will not make sense unless I can describe it unambiguously. I can't afford to stop the show while I draw a verbal diagram thirty words long; I have to cramp it into half a dozen words and keep things going forward, or the pacing will flag and the illusion of *motion* will be lost. It seems like a trivial thing, but every time you take ten seconds' worth of reading to describe an eyeblink's worth of activity, you strain your readers' patience and risk throwing them out of the story. Immersive readers are not a forgiving lot; you may make a hundred mistakes that they will never notice, but as soon as you make the one mistake they *do* notice, they are out of their trance and may never get it back again. Some readers will be bounced out by things that are not, strictly speaking, mistakes at all – matters of taste, things that call up associations in their minds that you could never have guessed or made allowance for. This is bad enough. The immersive *writer's* great and unending care is not to furnish the immersive reader with more excuses for bouncing out of the story and putting it aside.

As you may imagine, it takes a good deal of practice to wear this many hats at once – to be attending all at once to the movie in your head, the flow of your prose, the choice of individual words, and the *timing* of everything in the scene. To do it all in one draft is an extraordinarily difficult juggling act; I find I can only do it at the peak of my powers. I still do a good deal of revision afterwards: cutting, pruning, inserting bits of foreshadowing, rearranging scenes, and so forth. But if I don't get all the essentials of a scene to make it work on the first go, I never can manage to fix it afterwards. The structure must be sound or the building will not stand, no matter how many coats of paint I apply to hide the defect.

Since I can only do this for a few hours a day at best, and not at all on days when I am ill or distracted by other cares, I am not (by the standards of analytic writers) prolific. I keep reading advice from writers who think nothing of knocking off a million words a year, and prescribe career plans to other writers based on the assumption that if you don't write a million words a year, you are a mere piker or poseur, and will never find or deserve an audience. Such writers are either analytics or freaks of nature. Not even Ray Bradbury in his story-a-week days, or Isaac Asimov at his most fecund, averaged a million words a year. The complete works of Shakespeare are less than a million words all told. I am afraid that when I hear these million-a-year folk talk, I am seized with an urge to take up a different line of creative art, and express my cognitive dissonance by performing an interpretive knife dance on their entrails.

That, from my own point of view, is what it is like being an immersive writer – a certain kind of immersive writer, the kind that I am. I don't recommend *choosing* to write that way. But if you happen to be afflicted with a process that is naturally similar to my own, I hope I have given you some ideas on how to manage it a little more smoothly; or at least some company for your misery to love. And if you are not so afflicted, I hope I have given you a bit of insight into life on the other side of the fence, where the grass is only greener because we have painted it that way, blade by painful blade.

STURGEON'S LAW SCHOOL

THEODORE STURGEON is the sort of unfortunate author who is far better known for a single pithy aphorism than for all his books and stories combined. His brilliant science fiction is seldom reprinted nowadays, as it requires a certain sensibility and flexibility from the reader, and this is an investment that the big reading public just doesn't want to make. (It doesn't help that the publishing industry in general is doggedly averse to reprinting old books, but that's a rant for another time.) The average SF reader today has never read 'Microcosmic God' or *More Than Human*. If he knows Sturgeon at all, it's likely to be in the context of Sturgeon's Law:

> Ninety percent of science fiction is crud, but then ninety percent of everything is crud.

Many people nowadays say that Sturgeon was being charitable. And that 90 percent figure leaves out all the vast mountains of unpublished fiction, the stuff that is simply too cruddy for anyone to print. But the crud gets written, and some of it gets published, and hardly any of the perpetrators are aware that the stuff they're trying to inflict on the world *is* crud.

Crud happens. Why can't the crudsters tell?

In a rather animated discussion of this very question a while back, Mary Catelli suggested that the people who write crud simply haven't got the skills to tell it from the good stuff:

> What do you need to recognize horrible writing? You need to be able to recognize cliches, bad grammar, flat-footed prose, plot holes, bad characterization, etc., etc. If someone is incompetent at producing good writing, he probably lacks the skills to recognize it when he sees it.

Mary is an astute person and a pretty good writer, but I think she's missing at least half the answer here. It's well known that stupid people tend to overrate their own intelligence, that socially inept people tend to overrate their own social skills, and that everybody thinks he's a better driver than the moron he just crashed into. In the oft-cited article, 'Unskilled and Unaware of It: How Difficulties in Recognizing One's Own Incompetence Lead to Inflated Self-Assessments', Kruger and Dunning do a creditable job of analysing the phenomenon. But when questions of artistic value arise, I think something more insidious is at work.

So here's the 64-bit question: *Why do people with good taste create bad art?*

It's unquestionable that they do. There are people who admire the Old Masters, who can talk intelligently about Rembrandt's shadows and Turner's lights and Michelangelo's muscle fetish, but if they try to draw anything themselves, they produce something a kindergarten child's mother would be ashamed to post on the refrigerator door. Some people are connoisseurs of classical music, up on theory, familiar with the great composers, hip to the raging faction-fight between the devotees of von Karajan and the laid-back Viennese school of conducting, but cannot play a musical instrument or carry a tune in a bucket. There are those who know in their very bones that Olivier could act and Tom Green can't, but whose own gifts in that line are rather to be compared with Mr. Green's than Sir Laurence's, though strictly speaking they take a back seat to either of those worthies. And so it is through all the arts. As Kruger and

Dunning acknowledge, there are many abilities that you need not actually possess yourself in order to tell whether someone else has them.

If this were a sufficient answer to the big question, it would hardly be worth powder and shot. But another issue is involved. For some of these same people, those with well-developed critical tastes in their chosen artistic genres, are the very ones who blithely inflict the most appalling crud on the world under the delusion that they too are intimate with their chosen Muse.

Being the most readily available *corpus vile* for this study, and the only one whose permission to be pilloried I can easily procure, I shall offer myself as a bad example. Like most writers, I started off by writing a lot of wretched juvenilia: the sort of stuff that earns plaudits in grade-school English classes, but is strictly speaking not worth its weight in fish-wrap. One must start somewhere; and I knew perfectly well that my achievements were far short of my ambitions. For one thing, my taste was horribly undeveloped; I was still at the age when one can mistake Piers Anthony for literature. I had read good books, but not enough of them to figure out what it was that made them good; I had read clichéd third-hand hackwork, but not enough to appreciate the full tedium of a thousand-times-told tale.

So while my peers were coming to terms with puberty, I was scribbling in notebooks, or grinding out on a pathetically antique Underwood, pastiches of imitations of sendups of hand-me-down Golden Age tropes, and fondly imagined that the stuff I was writing was science fiction. I learned very early how to turn a decent sentence, and I always had a knack for visual description and 'atmosphere'. But my characters were something less than cardboard, and the art of drawing out a story to a dramatically appropriate length was a dark mystery. I wrote plot-summaries rather than narratives, vignettes rather than scenes, and all based upon the vapid conceits and recycled TV shinola that I mistook for ideas. In other words, I was a fairly typical twelve-year-old writer. I knew others like me then, and have met more since.

Now, I soon observed a thing that inspired me with melancholy, and would have led on to outright despair if I had not had the bumptiousness to ignore it. While I was writing my vile stuff, I thought it was pretty good, that the creative juices were flowing well, and that I was a talent that would be heard from at no distant date. Upon rereading my output in cold blood, weeks or months later, I could see it was the most appalling rubbish. And though my technique rapidly improved, this schizophrenic discontinuity between the act of creation and the brutal reality of self-criticism carried on undiminished right into my twenties. I had been writing with malice aforethought for ten years or more before I wrote anything that I could stand to read after an interval. How did this happen? My taste at 22 was vastly better than it was at 12, yet I seemed as far away from writing *good* fiction as ever. I can think of three processes at work, which, taken together, seem sufficient to cover the facts.

First, any creative activity, however badly done, is likely to be *fun*. The rush of inspiration, the pleasure of working at your craft, the feeling of *doing* something you have only watched before – these things bring you joy, even if the finished product cannot possibly bring joy to anyone else. Frederik Pohl hits it off perfectly in describing his work in an amateur press association. There was, of course, no Internet in the 1930s, when he was learning his craft; but there was cheap printing and postage, and APAs then filled the same niche as group blogs nowadays. All his life, as Pohl said in *The Way the Future Was,* he could vividly remember the feel of his apazine in his hands, the crinkle of the paper, the smell of the ink, the heady sense of being an *auteur;* but nothing at all about the actual *contents.* In a way, the contents hardly mattered. For art, any art, is first and foremost a toy, whether or not the artist is any good.

Second, most people develop early in life, and carry to their graves, certain habits of self-regard, all but unalterable by later experience. In my case, it was a habit of unrelenting self-abomination. When I was a child, the taunts of other children (those paragons of veracity and objec-tivity) quickly convinced me that I was ugly, smelly, badly dressed, ill-spoken, *etc., etc.* – and not only unpopular, but somehow *intrinsically* unpopular. Teachers and other authority figures reinforced this – most memorably, the one who informed me at full volume in class (this in a school built on the 'open area' plan of the Sixties, and therefore in full hearing of at least 120 kids) that I was a complete waste of space, would never amount to anything – 'and it's about time you realized it!'

One takes these things to heart, however unjust the accusations may be. I became thoroughly convinced that anything I did must be wrong, useless, utterly without value – simply because it was *I* who did it. I was not experienced enough to see that they were merely expressing their affection or hatred for particular persons, and disguising it in a thin veneer of critical commentary to give their emotional venting a bogus sense of objectivity. Instead, I came away with a profound belief that in some way the very same deed, done in the very same way, for the very same reasons and at the same time and place, might be a Good Thing if done by someone else, but was invariably Completely Wrong if done by me; and furthermore, that I was too stupid to understand the logic of it. For logic there must be; the people who rubbed these notions into me always took care to couch their abuse in the language of disinterested rationality.

Other people, of course, arrive at different pictures of themselves. I know some who cannot see the slightest flaw in their persons or their actions, and laugh off any criticism, however merited, as evidence of pure, petty, personal spite. The cult of unconditional self-esteem is as damaging to the critical faculties as the emotional firestorm I endured.

The point here is that young people tend to have an unrealistic idea of themselves as Good at some things and Bad at others, or as Good or Bad in all things equally, which, having never been based on facts in the first place, can hardly be contradicted by facts in the second place. By the time I began to develop as a writer, I was becoming aware of this tendency in myself. I knew that at least some of the horrible nausea that overcame me on reading my own prose was the product of my general self-despite. (I really did become physically ill when I read my work, and the sound of someone else *reading it aloud* was enough to give me panic-attacks and blind vertigo.) So I had a well-defined critical scale, but no way of calibrating it, or indeed of measuring anything between the extremes. It was just conceivable that my stuff was as good as it seemed to be while I was in the joyous throes of composition; equally conceivable that it was as horrible as my agonizing self-consciousness made it seem upon rereading. And I had no audience with the capacity to judge my work.

My first inkling of how to develop the skill of self-criticism came from an article by some well-known author, I have long since forgotten who it was, who said approximately: 'If I fall in love with a piece of my own writing, or if I hate it, I know that it stinks. It is only the stuff that I feel neutral about that turns out to be any good.' *Eureka!*

So I cultivated apathy and *ataraxia,* distancing myself from myself, until I found a sort of existential dizziness that worked as a substitute for objectivity. At that point, I had something to work with, a way of taking readings off my scale between the points labelled 'brilliant' and 'worthless'. I could, for instance, tell whether I was improving at characterization, or whether my plots were hanging together without requiring all the personages of the story to be blazingly stupid. But I was still missing one important thing: a *range-finder.*

This is the third reason why people show off their bad art in public. A beginning violinist knows she can't play like Stern or Heifetz. She can hear the difference clearly for herself – it doesn't take a trained musical ear. As her ear develops, she begins to understand how far she falls short of her models. But this understanding leaves unanswered two vital questions: How much more difficult is it to play like Stern or Heifetz than to do what I do? And can I improve enough to make up the difference? There are no obvious answers. Heifetz made it look so easy! But Heifetz had decades of painstaking practice and study behind him, and what's more, he was supremely gifted with that strange, indefinable, unquantifiable thing that some people call 'talent'. The distance between the young violinist and Heifetz is very great; it is almost certainly much further than she supposes, and she may well travel a lifetime without ever completing the journey.

It is the easiest thing in the world to dash off a story and send it to a magazine; far easier than joining a critique group, taking a course, or even applying one's own critical skills to revising and improving it. The only other thing comparably easy is to fool oneself (remembering the joy of creation, and knowing that one's critical self-perception is weak at best, and full of emotional baloney) into thinking that one is further along the learning curve than one actually is. When I first submitted a story to a magazine, I knew quite well that I was not about to put Heinlein out of business. But I had the idea that the progress I had made was much greater than it was. That story was something worse than worthless, and hardly deserved the form rejection it got. My second story, marginally less awful, got a personal rejection letter from the infinitely gracious and patient George Scithers, explaining in gentle terms why it sucked vacuum and how badly. After that, I gave myself exclusively to novels, with utterly indifferent success. I was only eighteen at the time; but on the other hand, I had spent *six years* working on my craft with the sole and specific intention of one day becoming a published author. I had made great strides since the days of my lost, unlamented juvenilia. But I still had no idea how long the journey would be. More than fifteen years later, I *still* didn't know for sure. But if I had known how long and tedious and painful it would be, I would never have set out at all.

This is by no means the worst fate that can befall a young writer. Undeserved obscurity can wither the creative faculties; but an undeserved *lack* of obscurity can kill them stone dead. Long after Fred Pohl's APA days, a young man named Jim Theis wrote a sword-and-sorcery story for an apazine, and made himself infamous for life. There is a widespread belief among science-fiction fans of a certain generation that his story, 'The Eye of Argon', is the worst piece of fiction ever written. This is not true; but it is at any rate one of the most inept works ever actually released to the public in the pre-Internet age. For many years, it was a standard party game at science fiction conventions for groups to take turns reading the story aloud: when you dissolved in helpless laughter, your turn was over and you passed the script along. Alas, the author was so mortified by this notoriety that he gave up writing altogether; if he had any more stories in him, he took them to his grave. This was a considerable loss to the world, if not to literature.

The opening paragraphs of 'The Eye of Argon' give a fair impression of the overall effect. Please try not to laugh:

The weather beaten trail wound ahead into the dust racked climes of the baren land which dominates large portions of the Norgolian empire. Age worn hoof prints smothered by the sifting sands of time shone dully against the dust splattered crust of earth. The tireless sun cast its parching rays of incandescense from overhead, half way through its daily revolution. Small rodents scampered about, occupying themselves in the daily accomplishments of their dismal lives. Dust sprayed over three heaving mounts in blinding clouds, while they bore the burdonsome cargoes of their struggling overseers.

"Prepare to embrace your creators in the stygian haunts of hell, barbarian", gasped the first soldier.

"Only after you have kissed the fleeting stead of death, wretch!" returned Grignr.

A sweeping blade of flashing steel riveted from the massive barbarians hide enameled shield as his rippling right arm thrust forth, sending a steel shod blade to the hilt into the soldiers vital organs. The disemboweled mercenary crumpled from his saddle and sank to the clouded sward, sprinkling the parched dust with crimson droplets of escaping life fluid.

The enthused barbarian swilveled about, his shock of fiery red hair tossing robustly in the humid air currents as he faced the attack of the defeated soldier's fellow in arms.

"Damn you, barbarian" Shrieked the soldier as he observed his comrade in death.

Let us skip on; passing over, for instance, Grignr's dalliance with a toothsome wench possessed (so the author assures us) of a 'lithe opaque nose'. A bit later – in 'Chapter 3½', to be precise – we are introduced to the artefact that gives the story its name:

At the foot of the heathen diety a slender, pale faced female, naked but for a golden, jeweled harness enshrouding her huge outcropping breasts, supporting long silver laces which extended to her thigh, stood before the pearl white field with noticable shivers traveling up and down the length of her exquisitely molded body. Her delicate lips trembled beneath soft narrow hands as she attempted to conceal herself from the piercing stare of the ambivalent idol.

Glaring directly down towards her was the stoney, cycloptic face of the bloated diety. Gaping from its single obling socket was scintillating, many fauceted scarlet emerald, a brilliant gem seeming to possess a life all of its own. A priceless gleaming stone, capable of domineering the wealth of conquering empires... the eye of Argon.

Bad as this is – and it is infamously bad, hilariously bad, with the delicious awfulness of an Ed Wood movie or a William Shatner album – it nevertheless shows evidence of skills learned at great cost. It begins *in medias res,* with a creditable attempt at scene-setting. The plot, such as it is, bears a sort of phantom resemblance to the standard 'plot skeleton' taught in how-to-write books: the same kind of resemblance that a five-year-old's Hallowe'en drawing bears to an actual human skeleton. It is recognizably made up of bones, or a plausible imitation of bones, though they are not connected together in any generally accepted way. The physical description of setting and action are actually fairly good; at least, they are not vague. Vagueness would have helped, perhaps. A good thick layer of muddy prose would have artfully concealed the silliness of Grignr's exploits with his fifty-pound broadsword, or the sheer primaeval stupidity of the 'scarlet emerald'.

In fact, 'The Eye Of Argon' is not utterly incompetent; it is haunted by a sort of sad ghost of competence. If it were not so good at reminding us of the effect it is trying to achieve, it would not be so killingly funny to see how it fails. It is a thoroughly bad story, but a readable one – even an entertaining one, if you approach it in the right spirit, like a paying customer at the World's Worst Film Festival. In fact, it is very like a thoroughly bad but watchable film. *Plan Nine From Outer Space* is one of the silliest and most incompetent films ever made, but one can see just why it fails, and what it is failing *at*. Contrast this with some of John Lennon's infamous 'art' films, such as the excruciating slow-motion picture taken by a camera flying through a cloud, or the extended close-up of his tumescing and detumescing penis. Those films are not only bad, they are unwatchable: even the poseurs who haunt the back rows at Cannes walked out of the cinema. Not even Lennon's most uncritical admirers professed to find them entertaining or instructive, and nobody but the filmmaker and Yoko Ono thought them artistic. It is the difference between a director who has some idea what a watchable film ought to be like, or at least could be like, and one who doesn't know and hardly cares.

If 'The Eye Of Argon' were fixed – if you cleaned up the execrable dialogue, and fixed the descriptions, and holystoned the prose till it contained no more scarlet emeralds or lithe opaque noses, and gave the characters motivations and personalities, and made the action scenes physically plausible, and replaced the pointless tomato-surprise ending with something that would actually resolve the plot, and generally attached some sense of importance and tension to the whole story, so that the reader could care whether Grignr achieved his quest or not, and was not fatally attracted to the alternative idea of how pleasant it would be to see him get run over by a bus – oh, yes, and if one applied some real skill to replacing names like *Grignr* and *Norgolia* with something a human being could read aloud and not be choked with superior laughter – why, then, one would have, not a *good* story as such, but a good bad story; a serviceable fourth-rate sword & sorcery story, the sort of thing that could have been published in any respectable pulp fantasy magazine of the 1940s; at least in an off issue, when the editor had to choose between printing substandard work and leaving a sheaf of pages blank. Good journeyman half-a-cent-per-word stuff, in other words, and better than a lot that was actually published in those days. Plenty of fan-fiction sites contain work worse than this.

It would be a colossal waste of time to try to fix 'The Eye Of Argon', of course, but it could be done. And that would not be possible if Jim Theis did not have at least a rough visceral notion of what constitutes a good story, and enough of the rudiments of writing skill to bring off a recognizable imitation of one. No doubt poor Mr. Theis composed his *parvum opus* in a white-hot fever of creative euphoria, and printed it in his apazine with maximum haste, giving him the best possible opportunity to repent at leisure. And no doubt he knew it was not professional-quality work, or he would most likely have sent it off to *Fantastic* or *Fantasy & Science Fiction* or *Weird Bloody Mighty-Thewed Pulp Stories,* and it would have vanished into the night with only the bare cenotaph of a rejection slip in the author's bottom drawer to remind us that it had ever existed at all. He just didn't know *how far* his work fell short of publishable quality, and so – he published it. It took a rare and fortuitous combination of lunacy and recklessness to give the world that tale, and fandom one of its most cherished legends.

QUALITY *VS* QUALITY

I N A CERTAIN TOWN that you have never heard of, though you may have lived there all your life, two restaurants face each other across a busy street. Both pride themselves upon the quality of their cookery; but if you read the menus posted beside their respective doors, and the little blurb at the head of each, you may come away with the idea that they are not using the word *quality* in precisely the same way.

The restaurant on the north side of the street has a bare white exterior and a bare white signboard, very chic in a thoroughly minimalist way; and on the signboard you will find this notice:

HOUSE OF MINUS
A Quality Restaurant
Minus Sugar
Minus Fat
Minus Sodium
Minus Cholesterol
Minus Gluten
Minus MSG
Minus Additives
Minus Preservatives

Minus Pesticides
Minus Impurities of Any Kind

The same bare white aesthetic is continued inside, with bare white tables and hard white chairs; and it is rather emphasized by the fact that most of the tables are empty. There are a couple of health-food cranks in one corner, and a lonely old man with digestive trouble sits near the kitchen door. In the middle of the room, a party of avant-garde restaurant critics are talking loudly, praising the wonderful geometric arrangement of the food on their plates, but not actually eating any of it. They can perhaps be excused for this omission.

For in truth, the food at the House of Minus is rather unappealing. The only thing on the menu is a special kind of digestive biscuit, manufactured on the premises, and carefully designed to contain nothing that could injure anybody's health or offend anybody's palate. The recipe was dictated by the owner, a self-made man who piled up millions in another line of work, and has convinced himself that sickness and death would depart from the world if only everybody could be made to live on an exclusive diet of these biscuits. Needless to say, he himself never eats there.

On the south side of the street is a bizarre building, as rococo as a wedding-cake, painted in all the colours of a fluorescent nightmare. If you shade your eyes carefully, you will be able to read the sign:

POSITIVE DELIGHTS
A Quality Dining Experience
Fusion Cuisine From Anywhere and Everywhere!
Thrill Your Taste Buds!
Astonish Your Friends!
Every Meal an Original Creation!

This, at any rate, sounds more promising than the Spartan fare across the street; but something seems not quite right, though Positive Delights is considerably busier than the House of Minus. Some of the customers are university students, visiting the place on drunken dares; some are tourists, steered this way by leg-pulling locals. A lot of people eat here once; but the place gets hardly any repeat business, for the delights, sad to say, are booby-trapped.

The cooking is skilful enough, for those of adventurous tastes. The chef has a way of combining the most unlikely ingredients and somehow making it work: it is the only place in the town, or perhaps any other town, where you can get barbecued sardines with a side of chocolate-coated garlic. And there are no words sufficient to describe the ice cream vindaloo.

But there is some question about the ingredients that he uses. Customers have a disturbing tendency to develop food poisoning, or go into anaphylactic shock. The meat dishes are rather suspicious. Small domestic animals go missing in the neighbourhood, and several customers have found dog-licences or bits of collar cooked into their dinners. It is a red-letter day when someone gets a salad that hasn't got insects in it. Nobody quite knows how the restaurant avoids the wrath of the local health inspector, but somehow it has stayed in business for several years.

Now, the really odd thing about these two establishments is that they actually exist. I have altered the truth in just one detail. The 'House of Minus' and 'Positive Delights' are not actually restaurants: they are writers.

More accurately, they are *schools* of writing. To some extent, they correspond to the analytic and immersive writers I mentioned earlier; but what really divides them, I believe, is whom they are writing *for*. When you are trying to use 'quality' as a selling-point, it matters very much what your customers mean by the word. Give them the wrong kind of quality, and you lose the sale. You may even enrage the customer, and in extreme cases, you can permanently damage your reputation. They dare not serve sticky buns at the House of Minus, no matter how well the sticky buns are made.

For the word *quality* is used in at least three senses, which have little to do with one another. Quality can describe the goodness of a thing, the attribute that makes it useful or desirable. The desirable quality of a light bulb is that it gives light; if it doesn't, we throw it away and buy a replacement. Quality can also describe the absence of badness or defects. If a light bulb shines for a few minutes and then burns out, we don't praise it for its quality, no matter how brightly it shone for that time. The third sense is more technical, used mainly by philosophers and psychologists, to mean any attribute whatever, good or bad. A light bulb has the qualities of brightness, warmth, and fragility, and so forth. In this chapter I shall try to avoid that third meaning, to avoid confusion. For the other two, I shall use *positive quality* for the good things an object has got, and *negative quality* for the bad things it has not got.

Much confusion arises because people hear the word *quality* used in one sense but think of it in the other. McDonald's restaurants pride themselves on their quality, a thing that scandalizes many people. That is because those people are thinking of *positive* quality. They think 'quality food' means food that is nutritious, tasty, or pleasing to the sophisticated palate. But McDonald's are talking chiefly about *negative* quality. Their recipes are boring and unambitious, and their ingredients are about the cheapest muck that can lawfully be served to the public; but they always follow their recipes to the letter, and their products always conform exactly to specification. There are no surprises, good or bad, under the Golden Arches. A Big Mac may be a mediocre hamburger, but it is never less than mediocre, and it is never adulterated. If you eat at McDonald's, you will never get sick from anything but the food.

Now how do we apply this to writing?

When we were very young, most of us, we had vivid imaginations and not much sense of probability or craftsmanship. We played at being cops and robbers, or cowboys and Indians, or Robin Hood, or Superman or Spaceman Spiff, and didn't care a fig whether we did it well or badly, so long as we were having fun. Adventure stories, no matter how poorly told, have a positive quality whose glow never fades. A bit later in life, we discovered that it was more fun to play our games by some kind of rules: if only to avoid the inevitable yells of, 'You missed me!' 'Did not!' 'Did too!' That introduced the element of negative quality to our play; and it is a necessary element, for it makes the game challenging. Superman is no fun when he can do everything; Kryptonite makes him interesting.

The schools of the industrial age, with their standardized classes and grades, squashed this quality out of most children by the time they grew up. To this day, some people still think that 'growing up' *means* losing the childlike quality of imaginative play. Perversely, some of them still place a high value on what they call 'creativity'; and they can go to extraordinary lengths to capture the *form* of creativity long after the substance has gone. They go to university to get degrees in Fine Arts; they enrol in Creative Writing classes and workshops; and there they are taught all the canons of good taste, and the rules of proper narrative, and the standards of rhetoric. Canons and rules and standards are good things, as far as they go: they ensure that the limits of *negative* quality are not violated. If you slip up when writing a story, and kill the same character twice, some of your readers will feel as much disgust as if you had put a bug in their salad. But canons and rules and standards are worthless by themselves, if a story has no *positive* quality to make it interesting and memorable. And no rules can tell you how to accomplish that.

It is true that Georges Polti wrote a book called *The Thirty-six Dramatic Situations,* in which he claimed to set out every kind of plot that can make a story interesting. But he captured only the forms and not the essences. His 'situations' are things like 'Supplication', which in turn have categories like 'Fugitives Imploring the Powerful for Help'. But any Superman comic has someone imploring the Man of Steel for help. If someone were imploring the police commissioner of Metropolis for help, it would not be such an interesting story, though a police commissioner is a powerful person. The story is not about any old fugitives, but fugitives from Lex Luthor the super-villain; nor about imploring any old powerful person, but *Superman.* The help required (and given) has to be worthy of the hero. He has to solve the problem by being faster than a speeding bullet, more powerful than a locomotive, and all the rest of it. You would not write a story where someone implores him to help them open a pickle jar or file their income tax. The 'situation', in the abstract, is meaningless; what matters is the specific problem, and the specific characters who have to overcome it. And that is not a thing that can be defined by rules or measured by metrics.

The things that can be captured by rules and metrics are either points of negative quality, or simple irrelevancies. The connoisseurs at Table Five, over in the House of Minus, are very good at coming up with irrelevant metrics. Last week, Positive Delights had a special on fried watermelon amandine with blue cheese sauce: a very interesting dish, to put it kindly. The gentry of Table Five tried to work out why it was such a success: they found that the dish contained eleven percent carbohydrates, six percent protein, five percent fat, and seventy-four percent moisture. But when they used that chemical recipe to reproduce the original entree, their failure was conspicuous and complete.

So it is with people like Polti, or the critics who talk knowingly about the Plot Skeleton and the Try-Fail Cycle. It is usual for the hero of a story to fail (or make matters worse) the first couple of times he tackles his problem. But there is nothing magical about *three* attempts. Again, the Three-Act Structure is handed down as gospel in certain quarters; but *Hamlet* has five acts, and *The Lord of the Rings* has probably about twenty, and I defy anybody to count the 'acts' in an eighteenth-century picaresque novel like *Roderick Random*.

Such writing rules, at best, identify frequently recurring patterns in fiction; but they can never account for the numerous exceptions. Still less can they be taken as commandments, or even as advice on how to fix an unsatisfactory story. A creature that has a skeleton does have advantages over one that does not. But you cannot change a jellyfish into a codfish by surgically implanting a set of bones.

Most critics, therefore, wisely leave structure alone and concentrate their negative criticism on matters of language. It is this habit or constraint that accounts for the 'sentence cult' I referred to earlier. Grammar is a thing that can be largely described in terms of rules, and rhetoric partly so. The tendency among critics, and (what matters more) among the sort of writers who play to the critics, is to focus on language, on stylistic monkey tricks, to the detriment of everything else. It is a truism in industry that you get more of what you measure and less of what you don't; and the same is true in literature.

Recall the passage from Annie Proulx that I quoted in an earlier chapter. This was praised to the skies by influential critics for its brilliant prose. But if you analyse what the prose actually *says*, as I was unkind enough to do, you find that the style actually gets in the way of the story. The event is simple and shocking: a woman's arms are cut off at the elbows by a bit of sheet metal. But the prose is not simple; the narrative is larded with figurative language and irrelevant description, which slows the action to a halt and bores the reader. The emotional impact of the event is not heightened, compared with a bald and simple account, but lessened.

One rule of negative quality is that it will not do to tell a story too simply or directly – a narrative should not always be 'on the nose'. Shakespeare follows this rule exactly as far as he ought; which is to say that he comes up with fantastic and vivid figures of speech, but cramps them into as few words as a straightforward account, or fewer. When MacDuff hears that his wife and children have been murdered, he neither states his feelings baldly nor gasses on about it for a paragraph. His grief and anger are distilled into a phrase: 'O hell-kite! – All? What, all my pretty chickens and their dam at one fell swoop?' The expression is vivid, original, and *short*, and therefore immortal. Proulx is not enough of an artist to be brief. In her desperation to avoid the obvious, bald narrative, she employs so much verbiage that the *positive* quality of the action is lost. You do not improve a guillotine by piling up embroidered cushions to soften the blow.

Fortunately for us as readers, we are not forced to choose between Positive Delights and the House of Minus. A book can have good positive quality – vivid characters, memorable incidents, or (as in Shakespeare) unforgettable poetry – without sacrificing the negative – competent prose and an intelligible structureq. On the other hand, there are thousands of books that fail by both standards. Positive and negative quality are pretty much independent qualities; you could represent them on a graph. Imagine that the vertical axis represents positive quality, and the horizontal axis, negative quality. These two lines divide the graph into four quadrants. Stories with good positive quality are high up on the graph; those with good negative quality are over to the right.

And now, to make the idea plainer, let us put some data points on the graph: let us read some stories. As far as possible, I shall choose examples that are well known to genre readers – books that are often reprinted, have been made into films, and so forth.

Quadrant I. *Strong positive quality, good negative quality.* Stories in this part of the graph tend to have great staying power. They may be famous or not – that is largely a matter of luck – but if they do win fame, it tends to endure. Readers tend to love these stories. Critics are more ambivalent. Some critics feel that anything popular cannot be good; and a fair number are simply suspicious of anything that their particular critical theory cannot fully explain.

The Lord of the Rings, as its author said, is one of those things. Modernist critics sneer at Tolkien's prose, but in fact he was a very skilful stylist – as I have tried to show in *Writing Down the Dragon*. He did not always follow the particular rules that govern negative quality in the twentieth-century novel, but then, he was not trying to write a twentieth-century novel. He worked in many styles, formal and informal, archaic and modern, to express the different moods and cultures of his characters; and seldom made a misstep or a technical error in any of those styles. Even when he breaks into rhymed and metrical poetry, the results are serviceable, if not brilliant. If you cannot abide any style but the flat Hemingway-and-water of the average modern novel, Tolkien will repel you; but if you have more catholic tastes, you can trust him never to throw you out of the story. In the matter of story mechanics, too, his negative quality stands out: the characters' motives are always at least plausible, their actions make sense in the circumstances, and we are never left without the information we need to understand what is going on in the story. These are considerable merits.

Of course, nobody reads *The Lord of the Rings* for its negative quality. It is the *positive* quality of Middle-earth that gets millions of fans to read and re-read the book, sometimes obsessively. The great positive mark of Tolkien's work is his fecundity of invention – or adaptation, since he borrows elements from old tales and makes them his own. He rescued elves, dwarves, and goblins from the scrap-heap of fairy-tale tropes, treated them with depth and sympathy, and gave them new life. Hobbits and Ents, of course, were his own inventions. Each of his invented peoples has its own history and folkways, and they are all interlaced to make a consistent pattern, grand in scope yet fine in detail. Thousands of readers have been fascinated by the background material in the Appendices, which could almost stand as a book in their own right: an almost unheard-of thing in Tolkien's own time.

If Tolkien is not to your taste, *The Princess Bride* has firmly staked out ground in the same quadrant. William Goldman is not exactly a poet, but his prose is crisp and effective and eminently quotable. Some lines from the book (and screenplay, which he also wrote) have achieved the status of popular proverbs. To this extent, his language, like Shakespeare's, crosses over from negative into positive quality. It is not merely error-free and competent; it has a flavour of its own, which brings his readers a special pleasure. The plot, though tongue-in-cheek, never contradicts itself or requires the characters to lapse into idiocy or blossom into infallibility; for good or ill, the characters earn their own fates. Where Tolkien turns the stuff of the old fairy-tales into epic, Goldman makes it into high comedy; and laughter has a positive quality all of its own.

It is, of course, immensely difficult to work in this quadrant; it requires the skills of a master. But it is not impossible, and as writers, we should be inspired rather than daunted by the possibility.

Quadrant II. *Strong positive quality, poor negative quality.* This is the domain of what George Orwell called 'good bad books': stories that 'have the curious quality of being well told and yet not well written'. Books in this category can easily become bestsellers, because they scratch some itch that is widely shared by the reading public; but they tend not to age well, and often seem ludicrous after a few years, when the itch is gone and the technical faults of the work are less easily overlooked.

Twilight is a famous recent example. The one overwhelming positive quality that Stephenie Meyer brought to her work is what used to be called 'sweet' romance. There were plenty of more or less pornographic stories about vampires lusting after live humans and vice versa; Anne Rice made a speciality of them in the 1990s. An actual *love* story about a human girl and a male vampire, in 2003, was strikingly original; and there was a large unfulfilled demand for any interesting love story not drenched in explicit sex.

The negative quality of Meyer's work is not good; there is much in the story that is merely laughable. Critics and comedians have sneered at *Twilight* for its sparkly vampires, with their bloodless hungers and sexless lusts. Her characters and settings have a kind of paint-by-numbers quality, her prose is serviceable at best, and the central conceit – that a century-old vampire is *still in high school* and has a romantic taste for teenage girls – is downright creepy in a way that the author never intended. While the

Twilight craze lasted, none of those faults mattered; millions of young girls, to say nothing of middle-aged mothers and maiden aunts (and even a few males), found nourishment for a starved and half-forgotten desire in Meyer's strange cross of horror story and soap opera. In time the fad blew over, and much of the audience recoiled from Meyer's sweet and sexless romance to the opposite extreme – and *Fifty Shades of Grey* was there to take their money.

Dan Brown's commercial success rested on similarly flawed foundations. *The Da Vinci Code* is sloppily written; it is filled with factual howlers, from the 'symbologist' hero to the Vatican's alleged corps of albino assassins; the characters act in wildly implausible ways, and the plot is driven by an alternation of coincidence, implausibility, and sheer idiocy. But millions of readers did not mind these faults, or could overlook them for the sake of the book's positive qualities. Brown produced a striking combination of thriller and detective story; the hero dodges bullets (and albinos) whilst solving clever intellectual puzzles, and the puzzles are set out fair and square so that the reader can play along. The book and its sequels are sheer intellectual candy, delightful if you have a taste for it, useless if you don't – and poison to a legion of critics, for whom the tasteless biscuits at the House of Minus are the only acceptable food.

Quadrant III. *Weak positive quality, poor negative quality.* It is not easy to find a good example of this class in written fiction, for the simple reason that such stories are not often published and read. Positive quality pleases readers, and negative quality appeals to critics; a story with neither is a hard sell. Magazine editors with limited budgets have sometimes bought such pieces, on the theory that a bad story is better than a sheaf of blank pages. Of course, an author can publish his own worthless work, and many bad authors do; but their books generally vanish without a trace, and nearly always without getting the kind of reputation that would make a story useful as an example.

'The Eye of Argon' is probably as famous as any *written* story can be whilst remaining thoroughly bad. In terms of simple mechanics, 'Argon' is a train-wreck. The grammar is unsound, the vocabulary atrocious; even the spelling is bad. The actual story is equally bad, an unmemorable pastiche of sword-and-sorcery tropes that were seriously worn out by the time Robert E. Howard died. I have quoted short excerpts in a previous chapter, and do not wish to punish you with any more. The negative quality of 'Argon' makes one cringe at its sheer, embarrassing badness; the positive quality, what little there is of it, makes one think of Conan the Barbarian or some other mighty-thewed hero, and laugh to see what a poor imitation Grignr is.

Quadrant III is a little better represented in film, because there are people who make a hobby of watching bad movies to laugh at them. Such delectable items as *Plan Nine From Outer Space* and *Attack of the Killer Tomatoes* belong soundly in this quadrant.

Quadrant IV. *Weak positive quality, good negative quality.* This is the domain of the critics' darlings. To some people, the lack of positive quality is an actual selling point. We all know the kind of person who thinks that any work of art must be bad if the general public like it, and uses 'commercial' as a term of abuse. Such people take refuge among their own kind; they are especially common in academia, where they can get a living for themselves by controlling faculty committees and sucking up to arts councils, and consequently don't need to appeal to an actual audience. Writers' workshops and MFA programs are notorious for teaching young writers to work in this vein; I have often heard editors complain about the number of stories they receive that are technically immaculate but completely uninteresting.

The same sort of critics who deplore *The Lord of the Rings* for its commercial success tend to be inordinately fond of books like *The Handmaid's Tale,* by Margaret Atwood. Of course, it helps that Atwood is in complete agreement with the prevailing (Leftist) politics of the critical and academic establishment. To some extent, virtue-signalling, repeating the right shibboleths and hating the right enemies, takes the place of positive quality in the tastes of the self-styled elite.

But only to an extent. Norman Spinrad is as Left as any critical theorist, but he also has a genuine knowledge and love of science fiction; he dissected *The Handmaid's Tale*, fibre by fibre, and tossed the bleeding scraps on the laboratory floor. To invert Orwell's phrase, this is a bad good book: it is well written but not at all well told. The prose style is excellent throughout; Atwood is a past master at catering to fastidious tastes, and there are no wrong notes to put the critics off their feed. But neither has the story any strong flavour of its own. It is set in a future America (one almost has to spell the name 'AmeriKKKa') in which the U.S.A. has become an evil fascist theocracy. The evil, of course, takes the form of a gratuitous and pointless sexual degradation of women, as the Wicked Patriarchs get their children on fertile (but lower-class) 'Handmaids' in the same bed with their sterile (but aristocratic) wives. But all this is a tissue of clichés, as old and tired as anything in 'The Eye of Argon'. The fascist theocracy was done well by Robert A. Heinlein in 1940, and done to death by many lesser talents thereafter; the evil patriarchy was a special *bête noire* of the feminist SF writers of the seventies – Joanna Russ, James Tiptree Jr., and the like. Atwood's sole original contribution was to couch this tired tale in pretty prose and – the key to the whole swindle – *not* sell it as a science fiction novel, but as 'literary' fiction. Atwood's audience of self-styled *literati* prided themselves on not reading genre stuff, and consequently did not know how desperately shopworn the key elements of the story were. —So says Spinrad; and I find that his verdict is substantially in accord with the facts.

This kind of pale but decorative imitation is much harder to get away with now than it was in 1985, when *The Handmaid's Tale* was published. Science fiction and fantasy are mainstream now; the big public play World of Warcraft and spend billions on superhero movies. A book and film like *The Martian*, which is the hardest of hard SF, is accessible to the masses now, and needs no Atwood to cleanse it of genre cooties for the literary crowd.

But there are other ways of playing the same game. One is to remove a story's *moral* cooties. Popular fiction, till recently, tended to be strongly moral and even moralizing, a positive quality that the well-bred critic positively despised. You can always curry favour and manufacture a sensation by inverting the moral compass of a beloved popular work. So Gregory Maguire stood *The Wizard of Oz* on its head, making the Wicked Witch of the West into a heroine; so Kirill Yeskov rewrote *The Lord of the Rings* with Sauron as the good guy. This version of the game has great potential still, and will probably continue for some time to populate Quadrant IV with books that are technically pristine, but thematically hollow and utterly derivative. The elements that give Oz its positive quality are reduced to dreary echoes in *Wicked;* the author of the pastiche contributes nothing vital or original of his own.

This, to the well-bred critic, is not a bug but a feature. Even the style of the parody can be inferior to the original. The critic will forgive some lapses of negative quality, provided that the positive quality (which his theory can never account for) is entirely removed. B. R. Myers said that 'sentence cult' critics can forgive a strong story provided that the style is sufficiently obtrusive; but they can more easily forgive a dull and slipshod style if the story is properly emasculated.

So what are we writers to do? Most of us (there have been rare exceptions) start out in Quadrant III, where we are good at nothing in particular. We hope (I presume) to end up in Quadrant I. But which road should we take? If we go by way of Positive Delights (Quadrant II), the *littérateurs* will call our work commercial trash. If we go by the House of Minus (Quadrant IV), the average reader will call us elitist, and ignore us thereafter. It is quite possible, even today, for a writer to earn a living by either of those roads; and to some extent our choice should be a matter of individual taste and inclination.

But I should caution against the House of Minus. The trouble is that negative quality, being describable by rules and shibboleths, is easier to achieve than positive: it is simpler to be error-free than original. This has two drawbacks. For one, the workshops and creative writing programs turn out hundreds of writers every year, all technically skilled, few of them particularly interesting; far more than the markets for that kind of work can accommodate. Success in that crowded field then depends on things hardly related to writing ability: personal connections, the right sort of background, and not infrequently, adherence to one of the smellier kinds of political orthodoxy. The worse drawback, however, is that once in that environment, you are liable to find little opportunity to improve the positive quality of your work, and still less encouragement. The House of Minus is infested with people who despise any strong positive flavour, merely because strong flavours are what the masses happen to like.

The dangers over at Positive Delights are equally grave, but easier, I think, to avoid. Nothing in the nature of commercial fiction *requires* you to write badly in the technical sense. Even the most philistine reader will forgive you for writing well, as long as you tell an interesting story. What's more, there are hundreds of editors, mentors, and how-to writers who will help you hone your technique. Every genre of popular fiction has its prophets, and some of them really do know the way to the Promised Land. But you need to choose your guide carefully. The moment you hear anybody say that technical skill is a *bad* thing, or even an unnecessary one, it is high time to stop listening and back away. Likewise with those gurus who insist that mere quantity is the sole and sufficient key to success. There have been writers who toiled away for decades, writing millions of words of trash, without ever finding or pleasing an audience. Fortunately, false teachers are fairly easy to spot; and because your success or failure is determined by *readers,* not editors or critics, the false teachers have no power over you if you choose to ignore them.

One more point: The very same gurus of negative quality who sneer at 'commercial trash' often reserve their highest praise for authors whose work was called commercial trash when it first appeared. In Shakespeare's time, the drama was considered lowbrow entertainment, and some of his early plays (*Titus Andronicus* leaps to mind) definitely belong in Quadrant II. Novels were *déclassé* when Sir Walter Scott and Jane Austen were writing their classics. Charles Dickens was a notorious writer of serialized potboilers for the mass market, long before the cultured classes discovered him and claimed him as a great man of letters. The literature of the English-speaking countries is largely the work of hacks and parvenus;

most of the great chefs learned their craft at Positive Delights before moving on to better things.

Yet modern 'literary fiction' insists on taking the other road. The great literature of the past, nowadays, is not very popular; literary fiction is not popular at all; therefore literary fiction is great literature. So the syllogism appears to run; and it is eloquent testimony to the badness of modern education that so many writers and critics think the reasoning is valid. (The particular error committed here, for those who may wish to know, is called the Fallacy of Converse Accident. Unpopularity is not what *makes* a work of literature great.) Perhaps logic itself is a form of positive quality. That, at any rate, would explain why it is shunned by the inhabitants of the fainting-couches at the House of Minus. There may be something in this. If there are two English books that are still widely read and loved in spite of being Great Literature, they are the *Alice* books by Lewis Carroll; and those books are *about* logic, in so far as they are about anything at all.

All said, I would rather take the low road of commerce than the high road of the *literati*. Norman Spinrad's twist on the words of Gilbert Shelton is, I think, a sound one: Plot will get you through times of no style better than style will get you through times of no plot. Let us tell interesting stories, and then try to tell them as well as we can; and leave the biscuit-eaters at the House of Minus to enjoy their substitute for fun.

OZAMATAZ

GOING VIRAL', the current form of overnight fame, is a kind of magic that can work on the most unpromising raw material. The comedians Keegan-Michael Key and Jordan Peele had their own sketch comedy series for four years, but their viral moment came from an absurd little skit in which they did nothing but make fun of the silly (and often self-inflicted) names one so often sees among American football players. The names grow sillier as the skit proceeds. It starts off with mild misspellings like 'T. J. Juckson'; moves on to delightful idiocies like 'Hingle McCringleberry'; and climaxes with outright dada names like 'Eeeee Eeeeeeeee' and 'The Player Formerly Known as Mousecop'. Of all the daft monikers Key & Peele introduced to the world, one in particular seems to have caught the public imagination: 'Ozamataz Buckshank'. The name *Ozamataz* has been 'repurposed' for any number of online game characters and social-media personas. I think part of the reason lies in the delivery. In the original skit, the name was pronounced in an intensely funny drawl reminiscent of Jimmy Stewart. It is, in fact, a *fun* name to say aloud, and I think that contributes to its popularity. But there may be more to it than that. Names like 'Jackmerius Tacktheritrix' and 'Javaris Jamar Javarison-Lamar' are too Pythonesque, too blatant in their silliness, to have much staying power. 'Ozamataz' is almost, but not quite, realistic; it could plausibly be an actual word.

And so, hearing the name again, I asked myself: If *ozamataz* were a word, what would it mean?

.

It is fairly clear, at least, how Key & Peele (or their writers) came up with the name. It is a portmanteau of *Oz* with *razz(a)matazz*. My handy Oxford dictionary app defines the latter word: 'noisy, showy, and exciting activity and display designed to attract and impress'. Oz, of course, was the name (or title) of the great and powerful and eponymous Wizard, whose magic consisted of little else but razzmatazz. Ozamataz must be the kind of razzmatazz in which the Wizard of Oz specialized.

Oz, by his own admission, was a humbug. He was, he insisted, a very good man, but a very bad wizard. This gave him an endearing quality that one does not usually find among frauds and con men. Dorothy and her friends very much *wanted* his magic to be real; and the Wizard's three bits of real magic all worked powerfully on that desire, and gave three of the lead characters their hearts' desires through a cunning twist on the placebo effect. The film, in this respect, is better than the book. Oz gave them *recognition* for the qualities that they actually had, but believed themselves to lack entirely: a diploma for the Scarecrow, a testimonial for the Tin Woodman, a medal for the Cowardly Lion. Alas, no amount of recognition could send Dorothy back to Kansas: placebos have their limits. But we leave Oz with the feeling that the Wizard not only meant well, but did well and even ruled well; even though his magic was three parts bluff and one part showmanship.

The American children who made up L. Frank Baum's original readership felt this quality keenly. None of Baum's other books were very successful, but children took Oz to their hearts. They loved the Scarecrow and the Tin Woodman precisely for the brain and heart that they themselves never knew they had; and they loved the Wizard for the very real magic that he could do, despite thinking of himself as a humbug. Literature is full of characters who are merely flawed. The heroes of Oz are heroic precisely because of the battles they fight to overcome their flaws – battles that they win, generally speaking, without knowing it.

Baum did not want to write any sequels to *The Wonderful Wizard of Oz*. It was the children who made him do it. After several years, he gave in to the overwhelming pressure of his fan mail (and the dead, gloomy silence with which his other works were received), and wrote *The Land of Oz*, a brilliantly successful sequel, and a comic-strip spinoff, which was successful without being brilliant. Still further delays followed before he began the long string of Oz sequels from *Ozma of Oz* to *Glinda of Oz*, the fourteenth book in the series. He then died; but Oz did not die with him.

On the whole, none of the sequels matched the quality of the first two books. At the time, Oz was something fresh: a joyous head-on collision between the traditional European fairy tale, with its trappings of magic and royalty, and the anarchic humour of the American tall tale. The first Oz books represent a spree of inventiveness never seen in either of those literary forms, and seldom rivalled in the fantasy genre of later times. After that, Baum had to ration out his creativity more carefully. Most of the later Oz books have glimmers of the original brilliance, enough (eked out with shameless recycling of the original material) to keep the fans entertained and the letters (and royalties) coming in.

The later books are somewhat spoilt by sentimentality. Baum kept dragging in the Scarecrow and Tin Woodman long after he had run out of things to say about them, because the children demanded it. In the fourth book, straightforwardly entitled *Dorothy and the Wizard in Oz,* he brought back the two leading characters from the first book, and completed the ensemble. Ozma taught the Wizard real magic, and Dorothy made her permanent home in Oz; and that, though it was just what the fans had asked for, killed them both. The *essence* of the Wizard is that he was a humbug who accomplished good and great deeds by clever fakery; the essence of Dorothy is that she wanted to go home. Without their essence, all that remained was a rather twee appearance. But if the fans of Oz could tell the difference, they were not experienced or critical enough to tell *why* the revived Wizard and Dorothy were less successful than the originals.

Baum's death did not end the clamour for more Oz books. The series was handed off to Ruth Plumly Thompson, who wrote more than twenty books in the series before tiring of her own formula. She gave it up in 1939, the very year that the film version of *The Wizard of Oz* brought Baum's creation to a new mass audience. The series was then continued by John R. Neill, who had illustrated every book from *The Land of Oz* on. Neill wrote three more books before his own death.

At this point, Ozamataz begins to resemble Ouroboros, the world-serpent biting its own tail. The next author of an official Oz book (after the hiatus of the Second World War) was Jack Snow, who had been a twelve-year-old Oz fan when Baum died, and became a Baum scholar when he grew up. The fans had captured the citadel; and they have been there ever since. In the 1970s, two more of Ruth Plumly Thompson's books were published by the International Wizard of Oz Club; this fan organization went on to print many more Oz books over the following decades. Most recently, Sherwood Smith's three Oz sequels have been officially recognized by the Baum family trust.

On the other hand, Gregory Maguire's revisionist retelling, *Wicked* and its sequels, has been officially snubbed, for good reason. The moral of *Wicked*, as of so much modern nihilist fantasy, could be summed up in a sentence: 'Evil is Cool, and anyway, it was forced to be Evil because Good is Even Worse.' This is a sentiment that Baum (like nearly all of his generation) would have regarded with plain horror.

And then there is the straightforward Oz fan fiction, not commercially published, and not officially recognized or deprecated by anyone.

We can say that Ozamataz, the peculiar fake-but-effective magic of the Wizard, leaked out of the books, made its tour through the lively century-long phenomenon of Oz fandom, and eventually came full circle as the fans grew up to write Oz books themselves.

In this wider or larger sense, *ozamataz* could be defined as the particular blend of creativity and publicity that inheres in a self-sustaining fandom, which has the power to call forth new work in the canon if the original authors cease to supply it.

Oz, of course, is not the only franchise with this kind of ozamataz. Sherlock Holmes was a still earlier example. Arthur Conan Doyle thought he had done with his famous consulting detective when he killed him off at the Reichenbach Falls; but the fans would not let ill alone, and forced him to go on writing stories about the resurrected Holmes for thirty more years. Since then, everyone and his dog has had a go at writing unofficial Holmes stories. The pastiches are beyond counting, from Sexton Blake to *House* and *Sherlock*.

Several of the modern media franchises have definite ozamataz. *Star Trek,* after the early cancellation of the original series, was kept alive by fan fiction, and Pocket Books' line of Trek novels became a stepping-stone for many young science fiction writers of the 1970s and 80s. Today, the *Trek* franchise has entirely escaped the *de facto* control, though not the *de jure* ownership, of Paramount Studios. Groups of fans from America to Turkey have produced films in the style of the original series, some as remakes of the original scripts, some with new material written for the purpose.

Doctor Who had a large and thriving fandom when the BBC axed the series in 1989; the novels and radio plays kept coming all through the show's 16-year hiatus, and in the end it was a lifelong fan of the show, Russell T. Davies, who brought it back into production. When Davies left the revived series, he handed it off to Steven Moffat, another old Whovian, who first came to notoriety as the screenwriter of the parody, *Doctor Who and the Curse of Fatal Death*.

Star Wars fandom has a more complex and ambiguous relationship with the creator of its franchise. In the earliest phase, the fans contented themselves with the strange ritual activity of watching the original film over and over, obsessively, often dozens of times – a substantial act of devotion in the pre-VCR era, when each viewing meant paying admission to the cinema. They collected the toys, posters, comics, and other merchandise, of course. But the real breakthrough came after George Lucas himself lost interest in his creation. Once it became clear that *he* would never tell us what happened after *Return of the Jedi,* a host of fan writers and young SF professionals brought us the Expanded Universe, more or less with the blessing of Lucasfilm. The Expanded Universe received a heavy shock with the release of the prequel films, which contradicted much of the fan canon. Many of the fans hated the prequels, but they accepted them as canon, and the Expanded Universe was reworked to fit the new official corpus.

Then Lucas sold the whole *Star Wars* franchise to Disney. The corporate entity known as 'The Mouse' first thrilled the fans, by announcing that Episodes VII through IX would be produced at long last. Then it alarmed and consternated them, by handing the job of directing Episode VII to J. J. Abrams, and leaking bits of story and casting information, which suggested that this would be yet another ham-handed Disney effort to cash in on a creative property that it might own, but did not understand.

Then came the war.

Earlier this year, The Mouse announced that the entire Expanded Universe was no longer regarded as canon. The slate is being wiped entirely clean. A new canon of post-*Jedi* stories is to be called into being, starting with Chuck Wendig's widely panned *Aftermath.* The far superior work of Timothy Zahn, as well as decades of writing and other creative work by countless fans, has been summarily dismissed. You could hear the screams of the neckbeards from Greenland to Antarctica.

So what will become of *Star Wars*? History suggests some possibilities that ought to give Disney pause. Several years ago, Hasbro, through its Wizards of the Coast subsidiary, made a similar head-on attack against its own customers. The third edition of the venerable *Dungeons & Dragons* game had been a resounding commercial success. Part of that success was due to the crowdsourcing of the basic rules. D&D 3.0 and 3.5 were based on the 'd20 System', an open-source rules set to which many hands contributed. There are dozens, perhaps hundreds, of tabletop role-playing games based on that system. Players can move freely from one setting to another without having an entirely new set of game mechanics to learn;

settings and adventures written for one game can be easily adapted for another. D&D benefited hugely from this creative cross-fertilization.

But the bean-counters at Hasbro were not satisfied. They wanted to recapture control of the D&D franchise, to make it their own exclusive property again. And the only way to do that was to abandon the d20 System and create a new, incompatible set of rules. This was bad enough; but Fourth Edition D&D was a conceptual disaster. All previous versions of the game had attempted to recreate the tropes and atmosphere of sword-and-sorcery fiction on the tabletop. D&D 4.0 tried to recreate *online* role-playing games on the tabletop. Instead of being a game about a fantasy world, it was a game about another game. And the complex real-time mechanics of something like *World of Warcraft,* which work smoothly enough when you have computers and server farms to do all the heavy calculation, are impossibly cumbersome when human beings have to crunch all the numberrs with pencil and paper. The Fourth Edition failed abysmally; and since Hasbro discontinued all the Third Edition products when it released the new system, the fans were left to twist in the wind.

They were rescued from this fate by a tiny startup company. Paizo Games released its own heroic fantasy rules based on the d20 System (which still remains in the public domain, available for anyone to use). *Pathfinder* is cleverly reverse-engineered to be maximally compatible with D&D 3.5, while introducing certain changes that tend to make the mechanics more elegant and streamlined. It is exactly what D&D 4.0 should have been. At first, Paizo did not even have the money to release *Pathfinder* in print; the original rules were made freely available for download as a PDF file. This was a stroke of genius. Thousands of disaffected D&D players switched to the free *Pathfinder* rules, then clamoured for printed and bound copies. That gave Paizo the pre-orders it needed to start mass production of printed *Pathfinder* products; and now, if you go to any tabletop game shop (except Games Workshop, which sells only its own proprietary kit), you will find racks full of *Pathfinder* products and a distinct dearth of D&D offerings.

It remains to be seen whether *Star Wars* fandom will reject the new Disney canon and cleave loyally to the old Expanded Universe. They have the disadvantage that nobody can reverse-engineer the original films. Disney will always have a hold over the fans through its control of the copyrights. But fan fiction and fan art operate in a world right outside the fences of intellectual property law. It may be that the ozamataz of *Star Wars* will be preserved through a kind of fan samizdat; that the really dedicated (and therefore profitable) fans of the franchise will tune out the official Disney offerings, and keep their own collaborative work as a separate canon in its own right. Or it could be that neither the Disney canon nor the Expanded Universe fandom will thrive. One thing is certain: The hand of Oz, the Great and Powerful, has been turned against The Mouse, and The Mouse brought it on itself.

I do not mean to give the impression that ozamataz has become exclusively a property of game and film franchises. The works of J. R. R. Tolkien exhibit ozamataz *par excellence.* Tolkien's story, in one respect, is curiously like Baum's. After the publication of *The Hobbit,* he was bombarded with letters from children wanting 'more about Hobbits'. But being a more serious and scholarly writer than Baum, and haunted moreover by a *legendarium* that he had been working away on for over twenty years, he was unable to tread Baum's path. He did not grind out dozens of children's books about the further adventures of Bagginses and Tooks, as he might have done. Instead, he wrote *The Lord of the Rings;* and the ozamataz jumped to an adult audience. The entire modern category of epic fantasy is the offspring of his work. The *magnum opus* was traduced on film through the efforts of well-meaning, if not well-informed, Tolkien fans, and so became known to hundreds of millions. At the opposite end of the media scale, a tiny but devoted coterie of fans write and publish pseudo-learned journals about Tolkien's invented languages. Nobody has yet got round the Tolkien estate's blanket prohibition on the commercial publication of fan fiction; but when Tolkien's copyrights expire, we shall probably see that as well.

A few other literary properties have ozamataz: most notably Harry Potter. One fandom exhibits the strange property of *anti*-ozamataz. The *Wheel of Time* had millions of readers, but did not attract a large community of creative fans; there is, I believe, comparatively little *Wheel of Time* fan fiction or fan art. This may be because nearly all the imaginative elements in the series were stolen from earlier and better writers, and any free play being done with those elements is happening in those writers' fandoms – most notably the fandoms of Tolkien and of Frank Herbert's *Dune* series. But the reverse ozamataz shows up very clearly in the Amazon reviews of the later *Wheel of Time* books. Nobody has begun a series with such lavish promises, or so blatantly failed to keep them; though George R. R. Martin may eventually come close. Beginning with about the fifth book, and with increased volume and stridency thereafter, Jordan's fans complain about the glacial pace of the story, the bad writing, the endless chasing of side issues and subsidiary characters. Hundreds of the reviews, both on Amazon and on innumerable fan blogs, end with the reviewer swearing never to buy another instalment; but all too often, that same reviewer will return to the series like a dog to his vomit, and make all the same complaints, with the same hollow threat, about the next book.

It reminds me of an old joke – speaking of dogs. An old Kentucky colonel was sitting on his veranda, sipping julep and greeting the neighbours as they passed by. His old yellow hound dog lay near him. Every so often, the dog would lift up its head and emit a heart-wrenching howl of pain and distress.

'What the nation is the matter with that dog?' a visitor asked.

'Oh, don't pay him no mind,' said the colonel. 'He's just a-settin' on a nail.'

'A nail! Well then, why don't he get up *off* of it?'

The colonel thought gravely about this. 'Well, sir, I reckon it only hurts enough to complain.'

Some fandoms are held together by admiration for a creative artist's work; some by emulation. And then there are those, like Jordan's fandom, or the *Star Wars* fans when discussing the prequels, that are held together by the shared pleasure of criticism, because it only hurts enough to complain. The one impulse leads to fan fiction; the other, to fan deconstruction. Both are legitimate amusements, I suppose; but I know which I would rather spend my time on.

The great trouble of any writer, in this world of sound bites and YouTube and virtually free publishing, is to stand out from the crowd; to get his work *noticed*. The traditional methods of promotion hardly work at all any longer, unless backed by (at minimum) the hype machinery of a major motion-picture studio. On the other hand, an obscure and unheralded artist may suddenly 'go viral'. When this happens, or at least, when it endures beyond the 'fifteen minutes of fame' prescribed by Andy Warhol, it is proof of the power of ozamataz.

The question, then, is how to *attract* ozamataz. Can one catch that particular kind of lightning in a bottle, or draw it down with a lightning rod? There do not seem to be any *sufficient* qualities to guarantee that a work or a franchise will develop a self-sustaining fandom. But perhaps we can identify the *necessary* qualities; and if we can work with those things in mind, we may increase our chances from zero to something that gives grounds for hope.

For it is the fans, in the end, who work the real magic when it happens. Would you know the secret of Oz, the Great and Powerful? Look behind the curtain, and you will find it: ten thousand geeks in hall costumes.

LEGOSITY

S O FAR, I HAVE DESCRIBED my thoughts about ozamataz to the point where I asked whether one could *attract* that kind of self-sustaining fan participation, and if so, how. This is also the point at which the Muse, or the Guardian Angel, or the Collective Subconscious, or Something, stepped in. Perhaps it was the Great Oz himself.

Having worked out something of the nature of ozamataz, I asked my brain: 'OK, brain, what is it that makes some things have ozamataz when others don't?'

And my brain, without missing a beat, obligingly answered: 'Legosity.'

I was duly annoyed, for I then had to figure out what *legosity* was. My brain is cryptic and has no manners, and seldom troubles to explain itself.

The one thing my brain did deign to tell me is that legosity has something to do with Lego. This made sense on the face of it. Lego toys have an ozamataz of their own. They have inspired movies, games, theme parks, and of course, the imaginations of millions of children the world over. The manufacturer's recent habit of producing specific single-purpose Lego sets like model kits, which hardly fit together with other Lego and are hardly intended to, is most regrettable. These kits tend to take up shelf space at the toy shops and displace the kind of Lego that you can really play with. But the original bricks and doors and windows, Lego people and Lego cars and Lego trees, and so on – those are still available, and you can do *anything* with them. Nowadays, you can even buy Lego with moving parts and electric motors, and build Lego machines that can be controlled via computer. There are Lego robots in the world, and serious men with doctorates in the hard sciences have been known to play with them.

As the unfortunate history of the kit-model kind of Lego shows, it is not so much the brand name, or even the mechanical ingenuity of Lego that gives the toys their unique quality. It is the *concept*. At bottom, Lego consists of a whole range of bits and pieces, all designed to fit together easily and without fuss, so that they can be used to build anything the imagination can conceive. You do not have to be a skilled carpenter, or a watchmaker, or know how to build ships in bottles, to make houses and cities and fairy castles out of Lego. The skill in your fingers (especially a child's fingers) ceases to be a limit on what you can achieve, and the mind is set free to soar.

Even the name *Lego* is well chosen, and means, I think, more than its inventor intended. We are assured that it comes from the Danish phrase *leg godt,* 'Play well'. But it is also Latin and Greek, and in those languages the word has a wide and subtle range of meanings that reach right down into the guts of the human psyche.

In classical Greek, λέγω means 'I put in order, I arrange, I gather': which are certainly things that you do with Lego, and indeed with any toy worth having. It also means 'I choose, I count, I reckon': the basic methods by which the creative process works on the raw materials furnished by the imagination. It means 'I say, I speak,' and even 'I mean'. And – most important of all, for our present purpose – it means 'I tell a story'.

Stories, in whatever medium, are more complex than toy bricks, for they have extension in time as well as (imagined) space. They *move*, within their own confines, or they do not exist at all. But the tropes and elements and imaginative bits and pieces that go into a story function very much like Lego bricks. You can spend years of your life inventing a monster that will metaphorically express the horror of death and the fear of lost identity; or you can dip into the barrel of Lego bits and fish out a ghost, a zombie, or the vampire's enslaved and unwilling bride. Every story ever written, probably, uses some of this conceptual Lego; for some of the pieces are older than writing itself.

If I wanted to make up a bogus etymology for *legosity*, I would pretend that it did not come from *Lego* at all. I would choose the Latin form, *lego*, which means 'I choose', and 'I gather', and also 'I read' (originally in the sense of reading *aloud*). I would make up an adjective *legosus*, which would mean 'well-chosen' and also 'worth reading'; from which one naturally gets the abstract noun *legositas*, which goes into English as *legosity* – and there you are. But I shall not dissemble. I got the word from my brain, and my brain got it from Lego.

Legosity, then, is the quality that makes an idea go easily into stories. Things that have legosity tend to connect together easily, like Lego bricks. They are adaptable and reusable; their play-value is not exhausted in one telling. There are thousands of stories about Robin Hood, and tens of thousands about vampires. Kings and queens, heroes and villains, monsters, perils, and things of nameless dread: these are some of the simple bricks that have gone into stories from time immemorial. They are conceptual Lego, and they are free for anybody to use.

Because they are free, they are taken for granted; because they are not original, they are not striking. They don't contribute to any story's ozamataz. *The Wheel of Time* contains barrels of conceptual Lego, swiped or stolen or recycled from every great story-cycle known to Western man: which, I believe, was the author's intention. But it has precious little originality. When you take it apart to play with the pieces, you find that all the pieces are somebody else's. From *Dune,* you have the secret magic sisterhood that controls the fates of families and nations, the Bene Gesserit (renamed *Aes Sedai*); and the shockingly *male* creature that sets the world on its ear by having access to the magic and ignoring the sisterhood, the Kwisatz Haderach (renamed *Dragon Reborn*); and the wild desert-dwelling people who have a hard-won lore of their own, with whom nobody can tangle and not regret it – the Fremen (renamed *Aiel*). From Tolkien – well, the very first page of Jordan's interminable saga mentions 'the Third Age' and 'the Mountains of Mist', and if that isn't straight-up theft with the serial numbers left in blatant sight, I don't know what it is. Nobody writes *Wheel of Time* fan fiction – at least none worth speaking of – for *The Wheel of Time* is itself fan fiction, in which all the fandoms collide together.

The works or franchises that I mentioned earlier, the ones that have long-lived and fruitful fandoms – the ones, as I put it, with ozamataz – all have this in common: they have *original* toys. They contribute new conceptual Lego to the barrel. 'Who can invent a new leaf, or a new story?' Tolkien asked – and then answered his own question, by inventing a whole botanical garden of new leaves, and resurrecting old ones that had been forgotten since the Middle Ages. It is this quality of primary invention – the *new* ideas, the *new* toys – that I shall refer to as 'legosity' hereafter. And I shall refer to the ideas or toys themselves as *lego*, with a small L, to distinguish them from the (trademarked) building toys.

The Wonderful Wizard of Oz, which has had ozamataz for more than a century, has this kind of legosity in abundance. Everybody in our culture knows the story of Goldilocks and the Three Bears; but few people know that the Three Bears were invented less than two hundred years ago by Robert Southey, or that Goldilocks was added to the tale at a later date (to its great improvement). Everybody knows the legos of the first Oz book; and everybody *attributes* them. The Scarecrow, the Tin Man, the Cowardly Lion; the Good Witches of the North and South, the Wicked Witches of the West and East; the Silver Shoes (which became Ruby Slippers in the movie, the better to show off in Technicolor); the Yellow Brick Road, the Emerald City, the Munchkins, the Land of Oz, and of course, the Wizard himself, hiding behind a curtain while he dazzles the world with special effects – all these things are part of our popular culture, and we know exactly where they came from.

You can go through each one of the works or franchises that I listed in 'Ozamataz', and identify the bits that give each one its legosity. When

I perform this exercise, I find myself marvelling at the sheer richness of our storytelling heritage – the vast and delightful variety of legos that our imaginations have to play with. So—

From the original *Star Trek:* the U.S.S. *Enterprise;* Starfleet and the Federation; Vulcans, Romulans, and Klingons; warp drive (very differently imagined from the point-to-point 'jump drive' then common in science fiction); phasers, photon torpedoes, communicators, tricorders; the transporter beam; the Vulcan Nerve Pinch.

From the original *Doctor Who:* Timelords and the TARDIS; regeneration; sonic screwdrivers; the Daleks, Cybermen, Silurians, Sontarans; the Blinovitch Limitation Effect, which is narratively important, because it sets boundaries on the kinds of paradoxes that so many time-travel stories have snarled themselves up in.

From *Star Wars* (the first film only): Darth Vader, droids, Jedi Knights, light sabres, Storm Troopers, the *Millennium Falcon,* the Death Star, jawas, dogfights in space, the Force, and of course Mos Eisley, the 'wretched hive of scum and villainy', of which the cantina was merely the most theatrical part.

From *The Hobbit* (leaving aside *The Lord of the Rings*): hobbits; Gandalf; Thror's Map, with its runes and key; the Stone-trolls; Elrond Half-elven and the Last Homely House; orcs and the Great Goblin; Beorn the skin-changer, the Eagles, the Wood-elves; Mirkwood, Lake-town, the Lonely Mountain; and of course Smaug the Magnificent, Chiefest of Calamities.

You can, I am sure, make lists of your own, from the fandoms you participate in, and from things you know to have ozamataz; and they will probably bear a fair resemblance to the five I have given.

Let us look over these lists a little more closely, and see what they have in common, and whether we can draw any conclusions from that.

To begin with, you may notice that the *lead* characters of each work are *not* included. There are several reasons for this. In fantastic fiction, the protagonist is often a sort of Everyman, a Jack the Giant-Killer (who is not a giant himself) or Alice in Wonderland – a relatively ordinary sort of person with whom the reader can easily identify, and to whom all the fantastic new inventions can be revealed and explained one by one, so that we can follow along. There is another kind of protagonist, the larger-than-life kind, who participates in the legosity of the story himself. Bilbo is a very minor example of this, for he is a hobbit, and we have to be introduced to the concept of hobbits; but he is so very much like a solid English squire of the nineteenth century, or the earlier twentieth, that *he* is encountering all the other marvels of Middle-earth for the first time, and therefore serves as our Everyman once we have got him soundly introduced. Sherlock Holmes, Superman, Robin Hood, are all examples of the larger-than-life leads.

Let us take Superman as an easy case to analyse. Much of the legosity of the Superman comics is embodied in the lead character himself; but he has to be unbundled. 'Faster than a speeding bullet, more powerful than a locomotive, able to leap tall buildings at a single bound': there we have three legos to start off with. Moreover, Superman can fly. He has X-ray vision. He is vulnerable to Kryptonite. He is really Kal-El, the last survivor (so far as we knew at the outset) of the catastrophe that destroyed the planet Krypton. He has a secret identity as Clark Kent, the mild-mannered reporter on the *Daily Planet*. We can easily take Superman to pieces in this way, and each of the pieces can be reused and recombined independently. So it is not the character of Superman who is a lego, but each of his salient qualities taken individually.

In the same way, Luke Skywalker begins as a farm boy, and only slowly learns to become a Jedi Knight. Dorothy is an ordinary little girl from Kansas before the cyclone transports her to the Land of Oz. Captain Kirk is thoroughly familiar with the workings of his own ship, but for the most part he discovers the new lego bits along with his audience, as he boldly goes where no man has gone before. It would seem that we can make a general rule: *Protagonists themselves are not legos, but their special attributes can be legos.*

What else do we find? Supporting characters can be legos by nature, either because of their *abilities* or because of their *kinds.* Gandalf starts off, in *The Hobbit*, as a lego by ability: he is a Wizard, and can do various kinds of interesting magic, and is moreover a kind of walking travelogue, who can instantly explain to the other characters what kind of trouble they are getting themselves into. (He had to go away in the middle third of the book, by narrative necessity. Having him around would have made things too easy for Thorin's Quest.) In *The Lord of the Rings*, it turns out that Gandalf is a lego by kind: one of the Five Wizards, the *Istari*, the messengers (angels, literally, in the etymological sense) from the West, sent to oppose the evil of Sauron.

Places and things can also be legos. Spaceships are a kind of generic lego; we use them without attributing them to any particular creator. But the *Millennium Falcon* is a new lego in its own right: the rickety, patched-together old smuggler's ship, not the least bit elegant or streamlined or futuristic – space travel's answer to the rusted-out jalopy. The Death Star, the space warship so huge that it can be mistaken for a moon, becomes an original lego by sheer force of scale. Things blow up in space battles, but the power to blow up a whole planet becomes a threat of a different kind. Mirkwood is a lego – the very name tells us what kind of trouble to expect there, and Tolkien delivers abundantly on its promise. Mordor, too, is a lego, the terminally diseased and polluted country, 'dying but not yet dead', where tormented nature is an adversary in its own right – the country whose very name sounds like *murder*. Lothlórien, the enchanted elfland where time stands still, is a lego, some of whose properties I have used for other purposes myself.

Technologies and 'magic systems' – a hateful phrase, for *magic* and *system* are two things that seldom go well together – are also common types of lego. The phaser is not just a zap gun, but a gun that can be set to *stun*: that is, a lethal weapon that, by a deliberate exercise of prudence or mercy, can be used non-lethally. The light sabre is not just a fancy sword, but the Jedi version of a Swiss Army knife: it can cut through metal or deflect blaster fire, and yet be safely and unobtrusively stowed upon one's person. The Force is a lego, and not just a fancy name for 'psi', because of its *quiddity*, its determinate and often inconvenient nature. A Jedi controls the Force, but the Force also controls him. It has a light side and a dark side, and if you make a habit of using the dark side, 'for ever will it dominate your destiny'.

There seems to be a kind of critical mass for legosity. To develop ozamataz, it seems, a work needs to have something like ten to fifteen good, solid legos that people will readily remember and enjoy playing with. This, I think, is what sets apart the major imaginative works, the ones that have their own fandoms and ozamataz, from merely successful books or films that never give rise to that kind of audience participation.

Some examples: The chestburster from *Alien* is a fine and memorable lego, but it is the only new lego in that movie; the rest is a recycling of common science-fiction tropes. You can easily play with chestbursters by combining them with legos from other sources (*Alien Vs. Predator*), but the world in which they originated does not have enough of its own legos to be worth playing in. *Back to the Future* has many fans, and several legos of its own – the time-travelling DeLorean, the flux capacitor, the 'Mr. Fusion' converter kit – but most of the story is constructed from existing pieces, so it does not inspire further creativity and has never really developed its own fandom.

There are, sadly, some properties that have abundant legosity, but have been blocked from developing ozamataz by some fatal flaw. A good cautionary example is *The Chronicles of Thomas Covenant the Unbeliever*. Stephen R. Donaldson is one of the world's great lego inventors. From the first book alone, I can think of a good dozen. Since most of my Loyal Readers are not Donaldson fans, I shall give a brief account of each, and what gives it the power of legosity:

The Land. This place, the setting of the series, is virtually a character in its own right; the whole country is almost sentient. It is a place where good and evil, health and sickness, are as plainly visible as red and green; where every tree and river, every rock and patch of soil, is alive with the organic magic called Earthpower.

The Council of Lords. This is not merely a collection of wizards, but a kind of church or mandarinate of wizardry, in which the leaders are linked by telepathy and by a common vow to serve the Land.

Kevin's Lore. Not just a 'magic system', but a very complex and weird set of what you might call magical scriptures. It was encoded by its creator in the Seven Wards, each of which contains the clues that will help you find the next. These Wards range from a locked box full of scrolls to a living being constructed out of pure Earthpower.

The Giants. These are not ordinary fairy-tale giants, not monsters or villains. They are a race of long-lived seafarers, who love to tell long stories, and to laugh even in the face of tragedy. Their motto is, 'Joy is in the ears that hear, not in the mouth that speaks.'

Stonedowns and **rhadhamaerl**. About half the humans in the Land live in Stonedowns, villages where all the tools and utensils of everyday life are made of stone, and manipulated by the stone-lore called *rhadhamaerl.* Even the fires are fuelled by a magical stone called graveling.

Woodhelvens and **lillianrill**. Woodhelven is a village built in the branches of a single giant tree. As the Stonedownors use stone for every ordinary purpose, the Woodhelvennin use wood. They even have wooden knives, which work because of the *lillianrill* magic that awakens the Earthpower in the wood.

Lord Foul the Despiser. The principal villain of the piece, Lord Foul is trapped in the Land, and wants to destroy it so that he can escape. Failing that, he seeks to torment the Land's people so horribly that they will destroy it themselves, just to put *him* out of *their* misery. He hates every form of life and existence, possibly including his own, and is very good at laying the kind of double-bind trap in which every possible outcome will result in his victory.

The Ravers. These three malevolent spirits have no bodies of their own, but work their will by possessing others. They can flit from host to host, using their stolen bodies to kill, destroy, and wreak havoc. The people of the Land call them by (Hebrew) names that refer to different aspects of Hell, but the Ravers name themselves by the (Sanskrit) words for different forms of enlightenment.

Ur-viles and Waynhim. These two strange races were created by a mysterious people known as the Demondim. They are outside the Law, since they were constructed, not born; their DNA, so to speak, is entirely artificial. The ur-viles are black, eyeless, and sorcerous, and serve Lord Foul because he gives them lore and genetic material to continue the Demondim breeding program. The grey Waynhim have renounced all that, and devote their lives to serving the Land in their own peculiar way.

The Staff of Law. This rune-carved staff both embodies and controls the laws that govern the Earthpower. It has, roughly, the power of life, death, and transformation over anything that exists by Law – that is, anything that has its own determinate nature. (Later on in the series, the Staff is destroyed, and Very Bad Things Happen.)

The Illearth Stone. A source of almost infinite power, the Stone warps and diseases everything it touches. It is a kind of Instant Mordor in a can.

White gold. This metal, not found in the Land, contains 'the wild magic that destroys Peace'. It is right outside of the Law; it is 'closed' to the second sight of the Land's people, so that they cannot perceive it as either good or ill, but only as an enigma.

These are all striking and engaging legos, with immense play-value; and the Covenant books, back in the day, sold millions of copies. Yet there is relatively little in the way of Covenant fandom, and hardly any fan fiction or other signs of ozamataz. Partly, this is because Donaldson himself is jealous of his creation, and has made it known that he does not like other people to play with his legos; and his fans, unlike those of some other authors, generally respect that. But mostly, it is because the Thomas Covenant books are flawed, and the name of the flaw is Thomas Covenant.

The protagonist of the series – you cannot possibly call him a hero – is one of the most repellent characters in modern fiction, and that is saying something. To begin with, a protagonist is supposed to be a character with a problem that he wishes to solve; but Covenant has a problem that he *cannot* solve, and he has invested his whole identity in the proposition that it is insoluble. He is a leper, and in the 1970s, when the books were written, leprosy was still an incurable disease; historically, it had the same kind of stigma that AIDS has had in more recent times. To help him survive, he has been trained in a rigorous discipline that puts physical self-preservation above all else. 'You cannot hope for a cure,' he is told. So when he is transported to the Land, where a cure is possible, he flatly refuses to believe in any of it. When his leprosy *is* apparently cured by Earthpower, he thinks he is dreaming, and rapes the young girl who gave him the cure.

This is the point at which thousands of readers threw the book against the wall, never to pick it up again.

For those who remain, the story becomes a dreary slog through Covenant's self-loathing and self-pity, occasionally redeemed by his efforts to save the Land. He is uniquely equipped to resist an enemy called 'the Despiser'; everyone already despises him, himself included. Lord Foul cannot manipulate him with despair, because he is already living without hope. This is ingenious, if you like, but it is also very depressing. The sort of people who build up fandoms and generate ozamataz, as a general thing, do not care for dreary and depressing stories. Most of them give up on the Covenant books before they even get to the fun bits. They are repelled by the lead character, and never find out about the legos.

So it does seem that the protagonist, who is never a lego in his own right, has a vital role to play in legosity. The lead character in a story or series, we might say, has to be a good playmate. He has to be someone that the reader *likes* to identify with; someone who plays with the legos himself, and whom the fans can imagine playing with them in different ways and combinations. A child can play at being Captain Kirk or Luke Skywalker. Nobody with a healthy disposition would play at being Thomas Covenant.

Of course, it is perfectly possible for a work to have a likable protagonist, clever worldbuilding, and a barrel of perfectly wonderful legos, and never catch on with the public. Examples are hard to give, for obvious reasons. *The Night Land,* by William Hope Hodgson, is an instructive case. Hodgson's very strange and arresting novel was published about a century ago, and unlike the Oz books, attracted no interest and virtually no audience. It did not help that it was written in a strange, mock-archaic style, weirdly at odds with the far-future setting. Still worse, it was a fantasy aimed at an adult audience just when Modernism was getting its literary grip, and fantasy was generally thought to be fit only for children.

But what legos it had! The Last Redoubt! The Watchers! The Air-Clog! The Earth Current! The Abhumans! The Diskos! The Night Land itself, where the sun has been extinguished and the earth is overrun by alien monsters, is a more powerful bit of lego than anything in H. P. Lovecraft. Lovecraft himself described *The Night Land* as 'one of the most potent pieces of macabre imagination ever written'. It deserved a following, and just lately, thanks largely to the efforts of the late Andy Robertson, and to the brilliant (and professionally published) fan fiction by John C. Wright, it has finally found one. But for a hundred years, it languished in obscurity, because it lacked one crucial element: *luck*.

To an extent, an author can make his own luck. This is far truer now, when anyone can publish an ebook and make it available to the whole Internet-connected world, than in Hodgson's day, when books had to be expensively printed, and distribution was difficult and dodgy. As recently as ten years ago, a book could go out of print in months or even weeks and be forgotten, seemingly for ever. But now we are living in wonderfully different times. The sheer overabundance of books (and films, and TV shows, and games) available to us is daunting. But we need not be daunted as authors; for our audiences know how to find us, if we know how to make ourselves findable. Other people have written more ably than I ever could about the problem of discovery; but I shall, I hope, have something to say about that, from my own angle, another time.

Meanwhile, I can say this with confidence: There is not much truth in the slogan, 'Build it, and they will come.' But if you can get your work discovered, it is quite fair to say: 'Make the legos, and they will build.' Legosity leads to ozamataz, just as surely as seeds lead to plants. Not every seed is viable, and not every viable seed falls on good soil. But every tree and blade of grass grew from a seed; and every fandom with ozamataz grew because a story had legosity.

THE EMPEROR'S NEW PROSE

I THINK OF SPIDER ROBINSON as a friend, as I do anyone with whom I have spent an evening harmonizing to the tunes of Lennon & McCartney. We're sharply at odds over politics and religion, but in considerable agreement on matters of what Spider calls *litracha*, and so I hope he won't object if I extensively quote somthing he wrote over thirty years ago:

> Considering how cerebral our genre is, it's startling how seldom you hear a reviewer say, 'I didn't unnastan it.'
>
> Perhaps it's precisely *because* sf is so cerebral these days, so hungry for serious consideration and academic respect, so desperately fleeing the drooling spectre of Buck Rogers, that we have blundered headfirst into the chasm of what my pal Steve Thomas calls the E.N.C. Syndrome. . . . 'E.N.C.', of course, refers to the emperor's new clothes, and the syndrome finds its most perfect expression in the statement, 'If I don't understand it, it must be Art.' *God* knows that sf is not the only art form to become entangled in the E.N.C. Syndrome – but it's right up there with the worst of 'em. Remember the *first time* you admitted to someone that you didn't understand what the hell was going on in *Dhalgren*? The timidity with which you

confessed to your English teacher that you couldn't make head nor tale of *Barefoot in the Head*? The secret shame with which you bounced off a Phil Dick novel? The uneasy suspicion that maybe you just weren't intellectually rigorous enough to grow, that the New Wave was leaving you behind with the rest of the lowbrows?

Reviewers in particular, me among them, will go to incredible lengths to avoid saying plainly, 'I didn't get it.' Perhaps we fear that saying this will establish us on some fixed point, *below* the upper levels, on the intellectual hierarchy, and thus disqualify us as critics. Surely a critic ought to be someone who understands everything?

Cow custards.

Now, writers of intellectual pretension use all kinds of monkey tricks to turn out stories that will baffle the critics into submission, but for the most part they rely upon three devices, which I now propose to mock. The first is the irrelevant allusion to obscure sources. In *Modern English Usage*, H. W. Fowler heaped scorn upon the semi-literate apes who afflict us with irrelevant allusions to the commonplace:

> There is indeed a certain charm in the grown-up man's boy-ish ebullience, not to be restrained by thoughts of relevance from letting the exuberant phrase jet forth. And for that charm we put up with it when one draws our attention to the method-ical by telling us that there is *method in the madness,* though method & not madness is there for all to see, when another's every winter is *the winter of* his *discontent,* when a third cannot complain of the *light* without calling it *religious* as well as *dim,* when for a fourth nothing can be *rotten* except *in the state of Denmark,* or when a fifth, asked whether he does not owe you 1/6 for that cabfare, *owns the soft impeachment.*

We all know people whose conversation, or what is worse, whose writing, is a kind of desolate beach littered with the hulks of unseaworthy clichés that have washed ashore over the years, so that it becomes nearly impossible to pick one's way along the strand. This is a tiresome kind of scenery, but not half so bad as the bizarre landscape produced by the literary specimen-hunter who specializes in raising ancient and forgotten wrecks to decorate his coastline with.

The irrelevant *classical* allusion was long favoured for this purpose, for tolerably obvious reasons. Until the late nineteenth century, English universities based their curricula soundly upon the classics, and derided the notion of granting a degree in English on the grounds that it needed no great erudition to master the merely vernacular literature. The would-be literary snob had to furnish his obscurities from Latin and Greek texts, or else be thought dreadfully common and uneducated, and so fail of his intent. This kind of curio-chasing had been going on ever since Hellenistic times, growing more self-referential and more Talmudic with each passing century; the pale final flowering of pagan Roman literature in the fifth century A.D. consisted of little else. Joyce, whose *Ulysses* is perhaps the most sustained and exhaustive compilation of difficult classical allusions in modern English, would doubtless have been grossly offended to be compared with the fifth-rate poetasters of collapsing Rome, but the comparison, though unfair in other ways, stands on its merits.

But once English literature received the approval of academe as a fit study for a liberal-arts major, the field was thrown open to the infinite variety of irrelevant *modern* allusions. Indeed, some Modernist authors seem to have earned their reputations chiefly by writing gnomic works alluding to sources not merely obscure but entirely unknown, except to an inner circle of cronies and simpatico critics. William Carlos Williams' most-praised poem, like Mona Lisa's smile, derives nearly its entire reputation from the fact that it is impossible to tell what it is actually about. As Dave Wolverton wrote in *Tangent* a few years ago:

The realist movement quickly developed a trend toward elitism, gaining a certain snob appeal, that I find very distasteful.

Under the influence of Ezra Pound, the imagists began writing in the early 1900s. Taking his cue from ancient Chinese monarchs, Pound sought to capture the essence of a story in one or two concise, overpowering images. Thus we end up with poems like this one by William Carlos Williams:

'The Red Wheelbarrow.'

so much depends
upon
a red wheel
barrow
glazed with rain
water
beside the white
chickens

Now, for those of you who have never heard that poem before, I beg you, what does it mean? Please tell me. 'So much depends upon' it....

Of course you can't figure it out by studying the text. The clues aren't there. This poem was meant to be appreciated only by a chosen literary elite, only by those who were educated, those who had learned the back story. (Williams was a doctor, and he wrote the poem one morning after having treated a child who was near death. The red wheelbarrow was her toy.)

Now, this story about the origin of the red wheelbarrow may be true, or it may not. It is at least plausible, unlike the reams of absolute drivel written by academics and critics who simply don't want to admit the obvious: that the poem is effectively meaningless, because it is impossible to identify its referents from the clues in the exiguous text. Perhaps the poem really does refer to a little girl's toy, and perhaps it refers to something else. It could even, as Julio Marzán insists, have arisen from a kind of bizarre topological transformation from another of Williams' poems:

> To arrive at 'The Red Wheelbarrow', Williams translated the relationship between Elena, the poet, and her physical surroundings into visual images. The soul-dead Elena, who held in her hand the empty pitcher from which she had poured out the regenerative vitality of water, is compressed into the idea of something on which so much *pende* ('hangs').

But the smart money is on Wolverton to win, and utter arbitrary meaninglessness to place. Henry M. Sayre notes: 'It is crucial that Williams's material is banal, trivial.' It speaks volumes for the pretension and phoniness of Modernist literary criticism that he actually means to *praise* Williams by saying it. Surely no emperor was ever so blatantly and admittedly naked.

In the very next paragraph of his article, Wolverton takes a potshot at Joyce's use of this kind of impenetrable allusion:

> Similar elitist fiction was touted as a higher art by James Joyce, who used voice rather than image to astonish his readers. Practically no one today can even understand, much less appreciate the ravings of Irish bar patrons in Joyce's tales. One student who complained to Joyce that he had read his works and didn't understand them was told, 'You can only understand my works if you spend your own lifetime studying mine.'

A study that no sane person, not even Joyce himself, would ever bother to undertake.

Sarah Dimento (whose drawing and design grace the cover of this book) once inflicted one of Brian Aldiss's lesser books upon me: *Report on Probability A.* This book was highly acclaimed by the SF literati in its day, for reasons that are now hard to understand until one knows just how slavishly devoted to E.N.C. Syndrome were the critics who praised it. On the back cover, I find these lapidary blurbs:

> 'A mindwrenching conception that forces one to question every common notion of human awareness, space-time, and perceptual reality' —*Tribune*
>
> 'Devilishly clever . . . . an exuberant imagination meets a passionate intelligence in this text' —*Guardian*

In fact, the only thing that a really critical observer would be led to question by this book is whether Mr. Aldiss was in full possession of his faculties when he wrote it. The story, if it can be called that, is ridiculous in the extreme. Three servants, a gardener ('G'), a chauffeur ('C'), and a secretary ('S'), all male, have been dismissed from the service of one Mr. Mary, presumably because they are all madly obsessed with his wife. In page after tedious page, Aldiss describes every least detail as each of them spies upon Mrs. Mary from his hiding-place in the outbuildings of the Marys' house:

> At present the face was in movement; it lay within the circle of vision of the telescope with its mouth at the centre of this circle.
>
> The mouth moved. The lips moved; the lower lip seemed to be plump, yet as it moved it extended itself slightly so as to seem less plump. These lips were viewed through six thicknesses of glass, four consisting of the little lenses in the telescope, one consisting of the square of glass that formed the central panel of the nine glass panels together comprising the round window in front of the old brick building, and one consisting of the openable but closed portion of the kitchen window. So near was this closed portion of the kitchen window to the moving lips that the breath issuing between them had fogged the pane....

And so on and so forth, *ad infinitum, ad nauseam.* It would be difficult to convey the tedium of this book in a short excerpt; it is all on just this level; in fact, Aldiss returns obsessively, over and over, to the deeply absorbing question of how many thicknesses of glass Mrs. Mary is being watched through. Yet he is incapable of attending to the most obvious details of internal consistency, starting with the important question of point of view.

Ostensibly the 'report' is a detailed write-up made by an observer from another dimension, watching G, C, and S, and trying very hard not to make any assumptions about their psychology or even their humanity by superimposing his own prejudices upon the bare facts. (Why did he not simply videotape the observing apparatus, thereby removing all possible elements of the subjective, instead of battling to record in writing merely the things he personally happened to observe? Only, one guesses, because then Aldiss would have no story to tell.) The watchers are watched by watchers from another world, who themselves are being watched, etc., etc. And as far as the plot goes, th-th-that's all, folks!

So we have occurrences like this among the watchers:

> Domoladossa pencilled a note in the margin of the report: 'She was singing.'
>
> He wanted to add, 'She was happy,' but that would be carrying the job of interpretation too far.

And yet this report, supposedly drawn from the excruciatingly objective observations of someone watching the physical movements of G, C, and S through an unspecified interdimensional viewer, contains whoppers like this:

> G's clock had been specifically designed to indicate the passage of time; it was his clock, for he had bought it with part of his wages in the days when Mr. Mary was paying him a weekly fee. On its face, which formed a circle, were the arabic numerals from one to twelve and a pair of hands. The smaller

of the two hands pointed at the lower lobe of the figure eight, while the larger hand pointed at the space between the nine and the ten. These two hands had been at these positions, maintaining between them an angle of fifty degrees, for a period of something over eleven months.

Now, we are told elsewhere that the watchers only discovered Probability A a week ago, and that events in Probability A have been moving synchronously with their own subjective time since then. How could they possibly know that the clock has been stopped for eleven months, or that G had bought it with the wages from his long-vanished employment? But it gets worse, for this nonsense immediately follows:

Although, when his attention encompassed the clock, G entertained the theory that the clock still worked, he was reluctant to test the theory by attempting to wind the clock mechanism.

This is probably the closest that Aldiss comes in this dreary book to attempting a joke. At any rate, I smiled slightly when I read it, it was so gratifying to see him unbend for a moment, remembering that he had readers, and condescending to give them a moment's entertainment. But if the author of the Report could tell all that about G just by observing the movements of his body, he was the greatest mind-reader that his world (or ours) had ever seen. His superiors had no such capacity:

Domoladossa thought, 'We'll have to decide.... I'll have to decide – whether these people have human responses.'

He even speculates that the very physics of the air molecules in G's world may be different from his own. In short, the whole performance is built upon an epistemological assumption that is casually violated on almost every page. It does not hang together, and the text is so excruciatingly boring that none of its parts are worth the trouble of hanging separately.

Now, maybe *Tribune*'s reviewer had a system of metaphysical beliefs so flimsy that Aldiss's tedious book-length jape could compel him to fling his philosophy to the winds. Maybe the chap from the *Guardian* really could find something 'exuberant' and 'passionate' in a 148-page description of aliens watching paint dry. More likely, I think, they knew that Aldiss was one of the Great Names in British SF at that time, and that to criticize him honestly when he produced a turkey would be more damaging to their own careers than to his; and so they praised the Emperor's *couture* to the skies, using the biggest lies that could be forced through the neural pathways to their typing fingers. In every generation, there are a few authors, perhaps a score, who are attended by a sort of halo of intellectual inviolability, and while it lasts, the critical consensus on their work is largely compounded of sycophancy, hagiography, and bollocks.

Now, Aldiss's obscurity is much less ambitious than Joyce's, though perhaps comparable to Williams', for it depends not on recondite references to works that only the elite have read, but on sheer boredom. Few readers could resist the deliberately soporific quality of Aldiss's prose long enough to spot the obvious fallacies underpinning the work. I would not have bothered myself, had not my friend so earnestly exhorted me to read it and form my own impressions. Well, Sarah and I are agreed: *Report on Probability A* is rubbish. But like 'The Red Wheelbarrow' and the rest of the arty-pretentious wing of twentieth-century literature, it is rubbish with an ineradicable patina of genius, for it, just like the pseudo-philosophical twaddle of Ayn Rand and Dan Brown, is *So Deep*. Which, as Spider points out, is often just a way to avoid saying, *I don't unnastan.*

HEINLEIN'S RULES *VS* AMAZON'S GAME

WHILE I AM TILTING AT WINDMILLS, I am minded to try a joust with that famous contraption called 'Heinlein's Rules of Writing'. What moves me to do this, chiefly, is the tub-thumping in favour of those rules performed a while ago by Dean Wesley Smith, who delivers himself of windmills and giants in roughly equal proportions. Someone ought to do the public a service and tilt at them all, and sort them, because it is not always easy at first sight to tell t'other from which. I have neither the time nor the stamina, nor probably the skill, to do them all, but I am willing to pitch in and take on a share if others will do the same. Since Mr. Smith is a great devotee of Heinlein's Rules, and often repeats them with greater force than clarity, it occurs to me that they would make a good target.

My peculiar taxonomy of windmill-tilting is, of course, one of the essential tools of human thought, an age-old distinction as famous as the sun, and has been universally recognized as such ever since I thought of it the other day. One part of the preceding sentence is true. In case it is the last part, I shall recapitulate, so that those of you who are new on the job may know what I am blithering about:

One of the jobs an essayist or a thinker can do is to play Don Quixote and tilt at windmills. Don Quixote did this because he imagined that the windmills were giants, which naturally needed slaying. Nowadays we have a tendency to take ideas as if they were expressions of unalterable natural law – predictable, automatic, and virtually infallible, like windmills; when they may only be expressions of personal opinion – capricious, organic, and mortal, like giants. So we tilt at them; we try to kill them, to see if they *can* be killed.

So let us sharpen up our lances and see if we can score a hit on Heinlein's rules. Here they are, as first formulated in a short piece 'On the Writing of Speculative Fiction', written in 1947:

1. You must *write*.
2. You must *finish* what you start.
3. You must refrain from rewriting except to editorial order.
4. You must put it on the market.
5. You must keep it on the market until sold.

The First Rule is non-negotiable; the only way to get things written is to write them. Frederik Pohl, in *The Way the Future Was*, tells a naughty story about a rich and cultured young Italian *contessa* who wanted to be a writer, and asked him for advice. She had the marketing and the byline all down pat, but whom, she wanted to know, should she hire to do the actual *writing*? The story is almost, but not quite, too good to be true. If you are William Shatner, or even Newt Gingrich, you can get a publishing contract on the strength of your name, and then hire a ghostwriter to do the heavy lifting. But the heavy lifting has got to be done by *someone*.

The Second Rule is one of those interesting things, a tautology that is not a truism. If a piece of writing isn't finished, it can't be sold; if it has been sold, it is finished as of that moment – with rare exceptions. (*The Hobbit* provides a good counterexample. The confrontation between Bilbo and Gollum, in its present form, was written ten years *after* the first edition was published; but it was so great an improvement, and so necessary to the sequel, that it completely ousted the original version from the canon.) But that does not shed as much light on real literature as we might hope.

When Mark Twain wrote *The Mysterious Stranger,* he hung fire a couple of times in the writing process; the last time, he was about two-thirds of the way through the projected story, and he never touched it again before his death. Yet just as it stands, the work ends at exactly the right place; no other ending could better emphasize its horrible and inhuman unity. Illusion after illusion is stripped away, and then the illusion of reality itself is stripped away: the narrator is left alone for ever with his own solipsism. When the story was published, several years after Twain's death, hardly anybody knew that the author himself had considered it unfinished. He was finished *with* it; and it was finished enough to make its point. It is not always obvious even to the writer when he finishes what he started.

Still, there is such a thing as an obviously unfinished story, and cases like Twain's don't come along very often. We can accept the second rule as it stands.

The Third Rule is where nearly everyone objects. On the face of it, it looks like a commandment to send out your first drafts and never revise them. This was poor advice in 1947; it was poor advice even in 1939, when the pulps were in their autumnal glory and Heinlein first broke in.

A lot of ink has been shed in vain to explain away Heinlein's Third Rule. One school of thought holds that what he meant by 'rewriting' was not redrafting and polishing, but tearing up a story and redoing it from scratch. Another says that he meant *excessive* rewriting, beyond the point at which the writer (somehow) knows that the story is ready to send out. Another – but it is pointless to multiply examples. The mere fact that so many people feel the need to explain the rule away shows that it needs some explaining. And it is nearly always on the Third Rule that Heinlein is attacked; though, as I shall try to show later, it is on safer ground nowadays than the Fourth and Fifth.

The fact is, I am afraid, that Heinlein *did* mean for writers to send out their first drafts, with the proviso that they should be corrected for obvious errors and cut to an appropriate length. The kind of rewriting Heinlein tended to do, at that stage of his career, really was *rewriting* and not revising; and he did it, for the most part, when he had reached a dead end in the story and had no idea how to get his characters out of their predicament. Then he would toss out the last part of the manuscript and cast back, a bit at a time, until he came to a point from which he could branch off and take the story in a different direction. But this, for him, was all in the course of writing the *first* draft.

He once allowed (approximately; I paraphrase from memory) that *Stranger in a Strange Land* took him eleven years and sixty-two days to write: eleven years of making false starts and then abandoning them, time and again, until he figured out how to tell his yarn about a Man from Mars; then sixty-two days of lightning work to write the draft. Once that was done, he sweated a good deal longer to cut it to 160,083 words ('and I am tempted to type those excess eighty-three words on a postcard'), knowing that it would be extremely difficult to sell at its original length.

This was Heinlein's normal method, exaggerated to the point of self-parody: write one draft, throwing away as many false starts and blind alleys as necessary; then correct it for grammar, factual errors, and stylistic infelicities; then cut it to suit the market. That is very little revision by the standards of most commercial writers; but even so, Heinlein was more fastidious than most writers for the pulps. I have heard of pulp writers who typed their *first drafts* with carbon paper – one copy for submission, one for the files. You don't do that unless you have the perfectly serious intention of submitting that first draft exactly as it stands. Sometimes, of course, one of these pulpsters would have to throw out a page and do it over; but not so often that it would have been quicker or cheaper to do a complete second draft and save the carbon paper for that. Some pulp writers schooled themselves to turn out 10,000 words a day, five or six days a week, for years on end; and that meant doing everything in one draft. Not many writers could put out 10,000 words in a day without degenerating into dada; hardly any could maintain that speed whilst writing two drafts, which (in the days when each succeeding version had to be typed out from scratch) meant doubling the work.

The pulps, you must remember, were the absolute bottom rung on the ladder of a writer's career. Good writers got themselves out of pulp writing if they could; or, at most, indulged it now and then as an outlet for stuff that they could not sell to a better-paying market. (In just this way, Heinlein himself sold occasional short stories to *Astounding* and *Galaxy* in later years, if none of the slick magazines would buy them.) Pulp editors were keenly aware of this, and many of them were willing to make extraordinary efforts to salvage stories. When Fred Pohl edited *Astonishing Stories* and *Super Science Stories,* his starting salary was a princely ten dollars a week; he paid his writers, as a general thing, half a cent per word. At that price, he had to buy a fair number of stories from amateurs, which meant choosing stories that were *almost* publishable and bringing them the rest of the way himself. Even John W. Campbell, Jr., though working with a much larger budget, used to brainstorm stories with his writers and then send them away to come up with a working draft, which he would then edit closely. Indeed, Campbell's relationship with his writers was much more like James Patterson's relationship with his numerous co-authors than anything you will find a magazine editor doing today.

Once Heinlein found the range with *Astounding,* he immediately became *two* of the magazine's star writers – Robert A. Heinlein and Anson MacDonald – with one appearance under the name Caleb Saunders. (Campbell didn't like to use the same byline twice in an issue; he also had a thing about Scottish names.) His stories routinely took top place in the 'Analytical Laboratory', the monthly readers' poll, earning him the magazine's top rate of a cent and a half per word. Anything that Campbell rejected – often for 'moral reasons', meaning that Kay Tarrant, his assistant, thought it was smut and would not let him print it – sold readily to other magazines at lower rates, under the name of Lyle Monroe. (Kay Tarrant was a force of nature. Another of Fred Pohl's anecdotes: Every writer in the *Astounding* stable was engaged in an informal competition to see who could sneak 'something bawdy' past her. Nobody succeeded until George O. Smith referred to a tomcat as 'a ball-bearing mousetrap'. This should give you an idea how tightly the pulps could be censored.)

Heinlein was too good a writer to *need* editing at the pulp level; once he learnt to avoid the faults of his earliest stories, not even Campbell could improve his work in any unambiguous and cost-effective way.

And the truth was that he was getting bored. He wanted to be up and doing, getting strenuous exercise, not sitting at a typewriter all day and worrying about his weight. He could have set himself to climb out of the pulps, but in 1941, respectable book and magazine publishers did not print science fiction and pretended never to have heard of the stuff. H. G. Wells, officially, was a Fabian Socialist writer and nothing else; Aldous Huxley, officially, was a kind of offbeat satirist. There was nowhere to go, as Heinlein himself said, but down.

When Campbell rejected Heinlein's story 'Goldfish Bowl', Heinlein took that as his cue to exit. Campbell panicked: his best and most prolific writer had just quit without notice. It took a good deal of pump-priming and feather-smoothing before he could cajole Heinlein into returning; and part of that process meant working out the minimum amount of revision that would make 'Goldfish Bowl' an acceptable story for *Astounding*. This was one of the few cases where the rider to the Third Rule – '*except* to editorial order' – had applied to Heinlein himself before 1947. (He would later do a good deal of rewriting to suit Alice Dalgliesh, his editor at Scribner's, compared with whom Kay Tarrant was a painted libertine.)

When he began selling to the 'slicks' after the Second World War, Heinlein found himself moving in a different circle – and one in which he was a great deal less important. He was famous partly for being the first pulp SF writer to sell to the *Saturday Evening Post*; yet he sold only four stories to that market all told, and had to work hard to do it. 'Space Jockey', his second story for the *Post*, was 12,000 words long in draft form. Heinlein took enormous trouble sweating it down to 6,000 words, the average length of a *Post* story, before submitting it. He then wrote humbly to his agent: 'I am beginning to understand the improvement in style that comes from economy in words.' He knew that if he had submitted the story at its original length, the *Post* would have rejected it for that reason alone; he *had* to rewrite without an editorial order, because the editor would not have bothered to issue such an order.

Nowadays, nearly all writers are in this position, which neatly destroys the usefulness of the Third Rule. You will occasionally, in some of the short-story markets, find an editor who likes a story but wants something fixed; and if you are an established pro, you may find yourself dealing with a book editor who dislikes your latest book too much to publish it as is, but cannot justify cutting you loose altogether. In those borderline cases, you may get an order to rewrite. Most of the time, you're on your own; most editors are far too overworked, in these idiotic times, to actually *edit* anything. Sometimes they are too busy even to read the books they are publishing: that work is left to assistants, or even left undone. And of course if you are your own publisher, as an increasing number of us are, an editor is a hired technician who goes over your work and suggests improvements for you to take or leave as *you* see fit. In such a case, there is no such thing as an editorial order.

What, then, is the self-publisher to do about revision? There is nobody to *make* us do it; nobody with the authority to withhold the longed-for imprimatur. Heinlein's Rules would then have us do no revision at all; and not even Dean Wesley Smith is quite that rash. I used to puzzle over this myself a good deal, until I found an answer that suited me. It comes straight out of the tradition that Heinlein wrote in; comes, in fact, from one of Heinlein's own heroes and role-models; and I am morally certain that Heinlein himself employed it in cutting down 'Space Jockey' for the *Post*.

Heinlein was an engineer, and surely knew the rule of thumb that used to be called the 'RCA Principle', but is nowadays known as 'design to manufacture': First build the best product you know how; then see how many parts you can eliminate before it stops working to specification. It is that elimination of superfluous parts that distinguishes a superior design from a merely adequate one, not only in engineering, but in art and literature as well. In this necessary skill, Heinlein's preceptor and mine was the immortal Rudyard Kipling. This is from his autobiography, *Something of Myself*:

> This leads me to the Higher Editing. Take of well-ground Indian Ink as much as suffices and a camel-hair brush proportionate to the inter-spaces of your lines. In an auspicious

hour, read your final draft and consider faithfully every paragraph, sentence and word, blacking out where requisite. Let it lie by to drain as long as possible. At the end of that time, re-read and you should find that it will bear a second shortening. Finally, read it aloud alone and at leisure. Maybe a shade more brushwork will then indicate or impose itself. If not, praise Allah and let it go, and 'when thou hast done, repent not.' The shorter the tale, the longer the brushwork and, normally, the shorter the lie-by, and vice versa. The longer the tale, the less brush but the longer lie-by. I have had tales by me for three or five years which shortened themselves almost yearly. The magic lies in the Brush and the Ink. For the Pen, when it is writing, can only scratch; and bottled ink is not to compare with the ground Chinese stick. *Experto crede.*

Writers nowadays are notoriously sloppy and prolix compared to those of fifty or a hundred years ago. Partly this can be attributed to the modern tools of the trade, which do not lend themselves to 'Higher Editing' with ink and brush. Even a pulp writer of the 1930s, as I mentioned, generally had to type his second draft from scratch before submitting; and that meant that every word passed individually through his brain a second time, giving him ample opportunity to repent. Writing on a cast-iron Underwood typewriter (I have done it myself) was heavy work; and at every word of the retyping, the writer's aching fingers would ask him desperately, 'Is this trip really necessary?' Sir Joshua Reynolds said, and Thomas Edison famously repeated: 'There is no expedient to which a man will not resort to avoid the labour of thinking.' But this is not so. A man will do the labour of thinking to save himself the deadly drudgery of retyping. Few things make me happier than thinking of ten clever words to take the place of fifty dull ones: a thing that often happens when I have to retype a manuscript from scratch. Necessity may be the mother of invention, but Sloth is the father, and he is more prolific than his wife.

The trouble nowadays is that we can be lazy without taking shortcuts; we are flooded with technological conveniences to help us achieve it; we can buy prepackaged sloth. The word processor is one of these conveniences. We no longer have to retype every word of a story in order to produce a letter-perfect copy for the printers (or the ebook file). What is worse, there is no visual cue to tell us whether we have even *read* a passage after writing it. The errors, infelicities, and excess verbiage of the first draft look just as clean and tidy as the niggling changes of the fourth revision. This tempts us to write in a sloppy, slapdash style, telling our story in the first words that come to mind and never bothering to improve them.

Our friend Mr. Smith recently informed the world that he had written 745,175 words of original fiction in the last twelve months. I felt tempted to ask him: 'How much was that *before cutting*?' It would not surprise me to learn that he had omitted that step, as Heinlein used to do in the bumptious days when he wrote his Rules. If so, he is robbing himself of the very best effects that his writing could produce. I will let Kipling deliver the sales pitch:

> I forget who started the notion of my writing a series of Anglo-Indian tales, but I remember our council over the naming of the series. They were originally much longer than when they appeared, but the shortening of them, first to my own fancy after rapturous re-readings, and next to the space available, taught me that a tale from which pieces have been raked out is like a fire that has been poked. One does not know that the operation has been performed, but every one feels the effect. Note, though, that the excised stuff must have been honestly written for inclusion. I found that when, to save trouble, I 'wrote short' *ab initio* much salt went out of the work.

Most Heinlein fans will agree, I think, that the period when his fire burnt hottest was precisely when he had learnt the art of cutting, and his publishers had not yet learnt that his books would sell by the million whether he cut them or not. Nearly all of his fiction from 'Space Jockey' (1947) through *The Moon Is a Harsh Mistress* (1966) qualifies as vintage Heinlein, a cut above what went before, and at least two cuts above what came after. It was the cutting that made the difference.

If you feel yourself moved to try this salutary technique, I may be able to give you some pointers; at any rate, I can describe the way that I go about it, in the absence of camel-hair brushes and India ink. After the first draft, I open two windows in my word processor, side by side, taking up the screen. On the left I have the completed first draft of my story; on the right, a blank document in manuscript format. I retype the story in its entirety; and as I go along, I invariably find improvements creeping in – better phrases, more vivid descriptions, quicker ways of moving the plot from A to B. If there is comic relief in the story, this is an excellent time to sharpen up the jokes and insert new ones. After that, following Kipling's advice, I let the new draft lie by for a while.

When I reopen it (by itself this time), I go along, sometimes using the 'Track Changes' feature in Microsoft Word, or its equivalent in whatever program I am using, and mark passages for deletion without actually deleting them. One pass will generally do for a novel, two or three for a short story; for it usually takes more than one pass to get a short piece down to the length that will work best. Then I make one last pass, deleting the marked passages, and making whatever small changes are required to button up the sentences so that the cut version flows smoothly and grammatically. At least that is the Platonic ideal of my method; I do not always apply it consistently, and with some kinds of work I scarcely apply it at all. These *essais* of mine, for instance, are dashed off almost exactly as they stand, and I do not cut them much, unless I find that an entire paragraph or section can come out.

Heinlein's last two rules are conceivable only within a solid framework of survivorship bias. The number of stories completed each year by writers in any given field has always been vastly greater than the number of publishing slots that exist in all the available markets. For most of those who conscientiously tried to apply the rules, it was not a question of keeping a story on the market until it sold; the most you could do was keep it there until you ran out of places to send it. Thousands of writers lived and died without ever making a single sale; thousands more sold only one story, and gave up writing before they figured out how to repeat the trick. Indeed, the 'man of one book' is a cliché in literary history. For every writer like Heinlein, who kept on selling original work for fifty years, there are scores like Daniel Keyes, who wrote an instant classic in *Flowers for Algernon,* and never came close to matching that success in the remaining half century of his life. Isaac Asimov, in his last volume of autobiography (*I. Asimov*), tells an unusually poignant anecdote:

> When I was handing out Hugos in Pittsburgh in 1960, one of the winners was 'Flowers for Algernon' by Daniel Keyes, which I had loved. It was surely one of the best science fiction stories ever written, and as I announced the winner, I grew very eloquent over its excellence. 'How did Dan do it?' I demanded of the world. 'How did Dan do it?'
>
> At which I felt a tug on my jacket and there was Daniel Keyes waiting for his Hugo. 'Listen, Isaac,' he said, 'if you find out how I did it, let me know. I want to do it again.'

But he never did. Keyes caught lightning in a bottle; and you can never count on doing that twice, no matter how perfectly your bottle is prepared.

Heinlein could speak glibly of keeping every finished story on the market until it sold; but he was, so far as I know, the only regular professional writer in the history of science fiction who actually did so. At one time in 1941, as he proudly announced, he had managed to sell every story he had written since he first tried his hand at professional writing – though he had to sell some of the stories at low rates to inferior markets. Nobody else that I know of ever managed it. Even Asimov died with seven of his earliest stories unpublished – permanently so, as the manuscripts had been destroyed. If there were an infinite number of slots for stories in the magazines, or if writers lived for ever, it would be possible for every writer to keep every story on the market until it sold. But the magazines are finite, and the writers die; and so it is mathematically impossible to keep Heinlein's Fifth Rule.

There is, nowadays, a clever workaround that *appears* to keep the rule. That is to self-publish your own stories. Magazines are finite, but the storage on Amazon's servers is effectively infinite: they can always buy more, and they never refuse an ebook unless they have grounds to think that selling it will get them in trouble with the law. If there is one thing Jeff Bezos hates, it is turning away a customer. So he will gladly sell your book, no matter how bad, even if the only person who would ever buy a copy is your own mother; for there are a lot of mothers in this world, and he does not want to see them take their business elsewhere.

But this is only an apparent workaround. 'On the market' and 'sold', for self-published work, do not mean what they mean in traditional publishing; they do not mean anything that even translates into traditional publishing terms. Traditional publishers accept a small number of manuscripts, and reject everything else. Retailers like Amazon and Kobo accept virtually everything, and then help their customers find things they like in the cornucopia. When you sold a novel to a book publisher in the old days, it meant that the publisher was confident of selling several thousand copies at the least; when you sold a story to a magazine, it meant that the editor believed the majority of his subscribers would be interested in reading it. (At least this was usually the case. Sometimes it meant that one of the magazine's regular contributors had blown a hard deadline, and the editor needed something plausible to fill up the blank pages.) But you can publish your own story without any assurance that anybody will want to read it; and in fact there are thousands of published ebooks that no one has ever bought.

It is this difference, I believe, that really points up the irrelevance of Heinlein's Rules today. The Rules merely described how Heinlein himself extracted the maximum amount of money and fame from the pulp magazine industry of his day. His system did not work for anyone else; was mathematically certain to fail for most of those who tried it. What it did do was give each one of his stories the maximum possible exposure, the best chance to make it past the gatekeepers and into the city of published fiction. Nowadays the gatekeepers are still there, but the walls have fallen down; the city is wide open, and we can stroll in whenever we choose – but that does not guarantee that we will do any business once we get there. The nature of the game has changed, and we cannot hope to play the new game by the old rules.

At best, Heinlein had the right answer to a question that nobody asks any longer. At worst, he had a wrong answer that happened to work for him, simply because he was too talented to fail at the game of pulp fiction. But that game does not exist anymore, and we will waste our time if we try to play it. That remains true even if a well-known writing guru refuses to admit it, and invokes the holy name of Heinlein in his defence.

CLOCK SHARE:
WRITERS *VS* THE COMPETITION

IN ONE OF HIS SERIES OF ESSAYS on 'Killing the Sacred Cows of Publishing', Dean Wesley Smith takes aim at what he calls the 'myth' that writers compete with one another. He pours scorn on this 'myth', and on all who believe it. A short but representative sample:

> The myth is simply that writers compete.
>
> Of course, this is so far wrong, it shouldn't be even talked about, but alas, it's still out there and going strong. In fact, I recently made the mistake of wondering over onto the Kindle boards and wasted a bunch of hours before I came to my senses. By the time I was finished with those hours, I knew I had to talk about this, since new writer after new writer talked about how they had to compete with all the other writers to get their books read.

He then goes on to paint a wonderful Technicolor picture of a world where there is an unlimited demand for fiction, pie for you and me and pasture for all the sheep, and the sky's the limit, baby. Now, I do not know what religion Mr. Smith adheres to, but I am a lifelong devotee of what Kipling calls the Gods of the Copybook Headings. And one of the

Copybook Headings, which people like Mr. Smith seem never to have heard of, is this:

Trees do not grow up to the sky.

Nothing in human affairs is infinite; no opportunity is limitless. It is true, and trivially true, that every invention, every industry, every product of human hands, creates its own demand. But it is also true, and trivially true, that this demand is subject to the law of diminishing returns. It is very easy to persuade most households to buy a motorcar. It is pretty easy (when there is more than one driver in the house) to persuade them to buy a second car. But once a family of three has four or five cars, they are likely to be keener on getting rid of a car or two than buying yet another. And if they live in Manhattan or Hong Kong, they may be rightly reluctant to buy even that first car: the roads are already so full of cars that they are very nearly stacked on top of one another.

Now, anybody who reads at all will desire a second book more than a second car. I have something over a thousand books in my flat, and am still buying more. I cheerfully paid money for my thousand-and-first book; I would not buy my thousand-and-first car even if cars were as cheap as books. We appear to have smacked up against the limitations of the analogy, so I hope you will pardon me if I abandon it for another.

Up to the 1980s, Coca-Cola and Pepsi gauged their success or failure in business by market share: that is, by the percentage share that each of them had in the total sales of non-alcoholic fizzy drinks. Then an executive (I forget of which company, but I believe it was a Coke man) came up with the idea of looking at their share of *all* drinks, even including water. Instead of resting on their laurels because Coke had (say) forty-five percent of the fizzy-drink market and Pepsi had only forty, he exhorted his fellows to get to work selling their product, because it had only about a five-percent share in the quenching of human thirst. He christened this latter figure with the incredibly ugly name of 'stomach share'. Both Coke and Pepsi have been hard at work increasing their stomach share ever since.

Now, we writers, considered in the aggregate, are in a somewhat similar position. J. K. Rowling and James Patterson, for instance, have each of them a considerable market share out of the number of copies of novels printed and sold each year; but compared to the overall market for entertainment, that whole market is one pip in a watermelon. What we need here is a word that expresses how big we are compared not to the pip but to the watermelon, as 'stomach share' does for the drinks business. 'Timeshare' and 'mindshare' have both been appropriated by marketing people for other uses. For my present purpose, I shall use the term 'clock share', which is at any rate less hideous than 'stomach share'; and if a better term is already in general use, I apologize for my ignorance.

The term 'clock share' has at any rate this advantage, that it suggests the division of the day into hours, and also suggests a pie chart: a symbol to which all marketers and stomach-share people are much addicted. It also has at least one important shortcoming, which I will deal with before going on. The fact is that, like some of those who consume fizzy drinks, avid readers suffer from anticipatory gluttony: our eyes are bigger than our stomachs. Some people have hundreds of unread books lying about, which they had every intention of reading when they bought them; yet they go on buying more. The number of hours one has in a day for reading is not a hard limit on how many books one buys. But it is, I may venture to say, a soft limit. We may buy more books in a year than we read in a year; we may buy twice as many; but if we buy ten times as many, our bank managers or our spouses, or at least the clutter in our rooms, will tell us sharply to knock it off. There is then some linkage between the number of books we read and the number we may wish to buy.

(Please note, also, that I am speaking of *trade* books, and especially of fiction read for entertainment. I myself have scores of encyclopaedias and dictionaries which I shall never read from cover to cover; but I bought those for different reasons. Reference books simply belong in a category by themselves, and I shall not even attempt to discuss them here.)

Every day, every human being (it is an astonishing equality) receives a free gift of twenty-four hours. A billionaire in Beverly Hills cannot buy or even steal a single hour from a starving child in Somalia. Out of those twenty-four, about a third are spent in rest and sleep; another third to a quarter, on the average, in work. To these claims we must add the minor taxes upon our time that keep our bodies whole and our civilization functioning: eating, washing, using the toilet, paying taxes, cursing the government, and (not least of all) transmitting these useful arts to our children. There remain, for the average person, perhaps seven hours a day that can be devoted to edification and amusement. That is the clock; that is the whole market, for shares of which we writers have to compete.

To some extent, we are also competing for money; but reading is actually a very cheap pastime. Orwell showed, in his essay 'Books vs Cigarettes', that even in the comparatively impoverished circumstances of wartime and postwar Britain, not many people were prevented from reading solely by a lack of money; they simply did not choose to devote much time to it as an entertainment. Every industrialized country today is richer than Britain in the 1940s; so are many of the countries that we persist in calling 'the Third World'.

Now, if every form of entertainment was equal, and people made their decisions solely by what was the cheapest way to fill the hours, reading would be enormously more popular than it is. Listening to the radio is virtually free; so is watching over-the-air TV. But both these pastimes are on the decline, chiefly because they leave you at the mercy of the men who decide what programs to broadcast. If you want to choose your own entertainment, you will have to pay for the privilege. An evening at the movies costs (in my part of the world) between five and ten dollars per hour. Live theatre, concerts, sporting events, and so forth tend to cost more, and fall into the bracket of luxury goods. High-speed Internet service, in these parts, goes for a dollar a day and up; for another $8 per month you can add Netflix. Or, if watching live shows (such as sporting matches) in real time is important, you can spend up to $100 or so on cable TV. A console video game may cost as much as $50, and provide anywhere from one or two evenings up to several hundred hours of amusement, depending on how open-ended the game is. The most open-ended games of all are the MMORPGs, which generally come with a monthly fee; you can amuse yourself with one of those for a dollar a day or thereabouts (plus Internet service). In short, leaving cinemas and live shows on one side, and considering only entertainment that is consumed in the home, you can amuse yourself more or less indefinitely for two or three dollars a day; more, if you want a variety of amusements, as most people do.

Where does reading fit in? The average literate person, I am told, can read about 300 words per minute; though people tend to read fiction somewhat more slowly, because they want time to picture the scenes and hear the dialogue in their own minds. Let us, then, knock that figure down to 200. Allowing for time to stretch the legs, fetch drinks, *etc., etc.,* and especially *etc.,* we may suppose that a middling recreational reader goes through 10,000 words in an hour. A doorstop bestseller in a cheap edition may cost about $10 and contain as many as 400,000 words; which works out to 25 cents per hour if you read it only once. Shorter books cost more dollars per hour, but then, better books may be worth rereading, and give you more hours per dollar. We may suppose that it all roughly averages out.

So, if all you do is read, and you buy all your books but don't bother with expensive editions, you can fill your leisure hours quite easily for the price that most people are willing to pay for online video games or cable TV. It is not a financially onerous hobby, as long as you don't mix it up with the horribly expensive and endlessly competitive game of being a collector. If you live near a decent public library, or read a lot of public-domain books, you can get by even more cheaply. I conclude that money, for most people in the richer countries, is not a significant obstacle. On price alone, reading can compete.

What competes is *habit.* Some people will sit in front of a television set for eight to ten hours a day, never getting quite bored enough to stir from the couch and do something else. Some people will play online games for stretches of time that nature never intended. And a few people, like C. S. Lewis in his palmy days, will, yes, *read* for ten hours per day.

I don't encourage people to do any of these things. But if one form of entertainment has 100 percent of a person's individual clock share, that's what it looks like. (Similarly unpleasant consequences can follow if Coke or Pepsi gets 100 percent of your stomach share.)

Very well, then: We don't want to conquer the world. We don't want 100 percent clock share. But there indisputably is such a thing as 100 percent clock share, and therefore, reading is in competition with other entertainments. Robert A. Heinlein put it with brutal simplicity: He described his job as writing stories that kids would read instead of watching TV, and that Joe Sixpack would buy instead of spending the money on beer.

If reading ever became the *dominant* pastime of literate people, then writers would indeed be in direct competition with one another for clock share. As it is, most people are in the habit of spending their leisure time on other things. It takes a particular kind of book to catch a person's interest and jar her into reading instead of watching *American Idol*, climbing mountains, knitting socks for the cat, or what have you. And the book that catches one person will leave another cold. Millions of people love *The Lord of the Rings* and reread it again and again; millions of others hate it and would pay to be excused. There are, believe it or not, even people who don't care for *Twilight*.

This will, I think, always be the case. The act of reading involves putting yourself into a mild trance state, and works well only if the physical and linguistic process of interpreting the words on the paper is largely automatic and subconscious. That requires effort. Then, too, storytelling actually involves a physical cycle of tension and release – the biological reason for stories to have plots. The upshot of all this is that reading takes *effort* – not only mental, but to a certain extent, even physical effort, and very few people will spend *all* their free time doing it.

So while there is a hard limit to the number of hours the collective human race *could* spend reading – about seven hours per day times the total population – the law of diminishing returns ensures that we will never approach that limit very closely. What we have left is a soft and squishy limit. Nobody can push beyond the hard limit, but a particular author, with a particular book, may get particular readers to push themselves far beyond the soft limit to reap the particular reward that suits them so well.

Now let us return to our muttons, and to Dean Wesley Smith's particular counterclaims. He goes on to say:

> So, let me take a hard look at the reality of fiction writing by dealing with the four things I heard new indie writers say over and over.
>
> Indie writers think they are competing against 1) other writers, 2) other books, 3) traditional publishers, and 4) the noise (meaning the crowding of so many books.)

Needless to say, Mr. Smith pooh-poohs all these claims. I think he exaggerates his case. Nearly all the truths you hear or read are half-truths, and most often the short half. Something is always left out when you try to express a truth in language, and the more complex and subtle the truth, the harder it is to express pithily. (Jesus of Nazareth's reputation as a philosopher, leaving on one side his status as a religious figure, rests largely upon his brilliance at expressing subtle truths in pithy parables. It's not as easy as it looks.) Consequently, if you deny one of these half-truths, you will probably be at least half right; but you leave yourself open to a just accusation of throwing out the baby with the bath-water.

Let us look, then, at some babies.

1. Writers compete against other writers. In general terms this is not true, since the clock share of recreational reading is so much smaller than it could be. In particular terms it may be true.

To take a trivial instance, I have often gone into a bookshop and wanted to buy more books than I had the money to pay for. I had hard choices to make, and each book I put back on the shelf represents an author who lost that particular competition. However, I am both a bigger reader and a poorer man than the average. Most people can filch enough from their beer money to buy all the books they really want to read.

TOM SIMON

More serious is the problem of competition for attention from publishers. In the Dark Ages, that is, the years up to 2010 or thereabouts, the only practicable way for a fiction writer to reach a substantial audience was by submitting manuscripts to publishers. Every reputable publishing house receives hundreds of times more manuscripts than it can possibly publish. The competition for slots on the monthly or quarterly list was always keen. Many an editor has had to turn down books or stories that she would very much have liked to buy, simply because there was no room for them in the publishing schedule.

For published authors, the competition is less numerically daunting but no less keen. The fact is that even within their lines, most publishers and imprints impose a rather arbitrary hierarchy. Each list has one lead title, which receives the lion's share of the promotion budget. Co-ops, end-cap placement, promotional tours, all the gimmicks that New York and London publishers use to shove books into the channel in quantity – these are reserved almost entirely for the monthly list leaders. The rest of the authors on each list have to make do with the leavings.

If you do reach the point where your books are routinely list-leaders, you are still not out of the woods. A well-known writer of my acquaintance was in the second tier of fantasy authors published by Tor Books. That is, his books did well enough that any new release of his was worth issuing as a leader, but not so well that he was in any danger of knocking Robert Jordan or Terry Goodkind off their tandem perch. It was, in effect, a matter of corporate policy at Tor that they should have two and only two superstar fantasy authors. My acquaintance had therefore to agree to a particularly odious clause in his contract, in exchange for the privilege of being a regular list-leader. He was not allowed to publish a book with Tor for six months before or six months after a new release by either Jordan or Goodkind. On one occasion, Jordan and Goodkind released new books exactly twelve months apart. That meant that this poor fellow could not have a new book out for *two solid years*. Two years is a long silence in this game; an author who has published nothing for two years will have a biggish job to do in winning back his audience.

The thing about these kinds of competition is that they are entirely artificial, imposed not by the nature of books or the nature of readers, but by the way that traditional book publishers choose to do their business. The bad news is that traditional publishers are continually thinking of new ways to make their business model even worse for writers. The good news is that they are no longer the only game in town, and we can bypass them entirely if we are willing to make the effort and take the risk.

2. Books compete against other books. Again, this is true only in specific instances; and much truer of nonfiction than of fiction. A book on a subject, especially a highly specialized technical subject, can be so definitive that there is no room left for a would-be competitor. In my own pet hobby of Indo-European historical linguistics, the definitive reference work is Pokorny's *Indogermanisches etymologisches Wörterbuch*. It is over 50 years old now, and showing its age, but the overwhelming effort of compiling a replacement, then selling it to the universities and scholars that have invested heavily in Pokorny, has so far been simply prohibitive.

Fortunately, writers of fiction do not have that to contend with. One story does not supersede another. My taste for *Don Quixote* does not inhibit my appetite for *Gulliver's Travels*. Rather the opposite: when a reader develops a real liking for something, she wants more of it than any one writer can provide. Amanda Hocking grew rich feeding the very audience that Stephenie Meyer could not sate. Isaac Asimov wrote five hundred books in his time, but there never was a reader who read all of his books and none by anybody else.

Again, what competition exists is largely artificial and arbitrary. One book competes with another for limited shelf space in brick-and-mortar bookshops – but Amazon's shelf space, being virtual, is infinite. One book competes with another for the limited printing, warehousing, and marketing budgets of a particular publishing house – but it is trivially easy to start up a new house. And with ebooks, the problem very nearly disappears. (It is replaced by another, perhaps more intractable problem – but I will come back to that in a moment.)

3. Independent writers are in competition with traditional publishing. This used to be true, because the major corporate publishers – the Big Five, as they now are in New York, though in the days of their real power there were more – tried to operate as an oligopoly and a cartel. They exerted their muscle to exclude small presses and self-published authors from Ingram's and the other major distribution channels; to keep them out of the New York *Times* and the *New York Review of Books*; to keep them out of chain bookshops and off bestseller lists.

There was a real and bitter competition between the big corporate publishers and the smaller presses; but that competition is over, and while Goliath is not dead, David has clearly won. Nobody thinks any longer that a book must be worthless because it is published by a small press, and few people can even keep up the old prejudice against self-publishing. Twenty years ago, a self-published novel meant a novel that no real publisher would touch, and a deluded fool with a basement full of unsold books. Today, it may mean a self-made millionaire like James Patterson or the aforementioned Ms. Hocking. A New York colophon was never a guarantee of quality; today, we cannot even pretend that the absence of a New York colophon guarantees a lack of quality.

4. Writers are competing against the noise. This is the modern replacement for numbers 1 and 2 above. It is certainly true that enormous numbers of self-published books have burst upon the market, most of them drearily bad. The slush pile is out in the open. This is both good and bad. The bad news is that readers now have to do the job that editors used to do, searching through the slush for things worth reading. The good news is that they are no longer prevented from choosing the books *they* want, just because the author could not find an editor who shared that taste.

A decade ago, I heard Mr. Tom Doherty, founder of Tor Books, explain the factors that cause readers to buy a particular book. The most important factor, as I recall, driving about 30 percent of sales, was the author's name: people who like one of an author's books very often want to try the others. Word of mouth and the actual book cover were the next two on the list, and all other factors combined – reviews, co-ops, book tours, author interviews, *etc., etc.* – amounted to perhaps 25 percent. (Mr. Doherty told me these things in a casual conversation, and I did not note down the exact figures.)

For self-published books, which are likely to be ebooks, the cover is perhaps less important; but the three main ways that a reader finds a book to buy are the same online as in traditional print.

1. Janet Stubbs reads a book by Helen Sweetstory and likes it. She goes out looking for other books by Helen Sweetstory.
2. Janet Stubbs tells her friend Joe Bloggs about this wonderful book she has just read. Joe is sufficiently interested to give Helen Sweetstory a try.
3. Janet Stubbs is browsing in a bookshop, and sees an interesting-looking book. The cover catches her eye, the title is intriguing. Approaching a little closer, she finds the blurb appealing. She leafs through the first pages, seeing how the story begins and what Helen Sweetstory's voice 'sounds' like. Having sufficiently kicked the tires, she decides to buy.

Of course, the online retailers have given us a kind of hybrid between 2 and 3, with the 'You might also like' feature. In effect, the virtual bookshop contains a whole section of books constructed on the fly for each customer's amusement. We may go traipsing over a physical bookshop for hours looking for something of interest, but for all the technical wizardry of Amazon, virtual traipsing is not yet an option. So instead we have a charming throwback to the days when a travelling pedlar would spread out his wares in the customer's home, selecting from his stock the things he thought she would be most likely to buy.

Now, if you are a brand-new writer with only one title on the shelf, you may never overcome the noise; but that is because you *are* the noise. The signal consists of good books and consistently good writers. Each time someone buys one of your books, the virtual pedlar takes note and begins offering that book to customers with similar tastes. Each time someone tells a friend about one of your books, or writes a review in his blog, the signal is repeated and grows stronger. And each time you come out with a new book, you have added a potential starting point at which people can notice you for the first time, and another product for all your existing readers to come back and (we hope) buy.

In effect, 'People who buy this book also bought', and the system of reader reviews at Amazon and other online shops, are ways to crowdsource the slush pile, and very ingenious ones. The recent history of the software industry shows that crowdsourcing is a highly efficient way to detect and correct errors; and from the standpoint of publishing, a worthless book is an error. In terms of information theory, it's all a matter of filtering noise.

The big losers in all this, perhaps, will be writers like J. D. Salinger or Joseph Heller, who were essentially men of one book. It was never very often that one book made a career; now it is bound to get even rarer. The filters cannot tell if you, the first-time author with a single new title in the system, have written *Catch-22* (which millions of people will love) or *What I Did Last Summer* (which your mother will pretend to love). Thousands of sheer and intentional amateurs are flooding Kindle and Smashwords and Createspace with the kind of books that they would once have sent to a vanity press. This is advantageous for them, since they no longer get stuck with that basement full of unsold books; not so good for the rest of us, and very bad indeed for the Salingers and Hellers of the world. For the present, it is still possible to boost your signal above the noise with one book, by selling it to a prestigious New York or London publisher. If you really are a man of one book, or such a slow writer that your second book will be long in coming, you might even now be well advised to avoid the noisy signal and do things the old-fashioned way.

Whether you pursue your readers by the old method or the new, the goal remains the same. We are all competing for clock share. First our work has to be worth our audience's time; only then can we talk about trying to get some of their money.

WHY I WRITE

From a very early age, perhaps the age of five or six, I knew that when I grew up I should be a writer. Between the ages of about seventeen and twenty-four I tried to abandon this idea, but I did so with the consciousness that I was outraging my true nature and that sooner or later I should have to settle down and write books.

I was the middle child of three, but there was a gap of five years on either side, and I barely saw my father before I was eight. For this and other reasons I was somewhat lonely, and I soon developed disagreeable mannerisms which made me unpopular throughout my schooldays. I had the lonely child's habit of making up stories and holding conversations with imaginary persons, and I think from the very start my literary ambitions were mixed up with the feeling of being isolated and undervalued. I knew that I had a facility with words and a power of facing unpleasant facts, and I felt that this created a sort of private world in which I could get my own back for my failure in everyday life.

—*George Orwell, 'Why I Write'*

I WAS NOT AS PRECOCIOUS as Orwell; I did not definitely conceive the idea of becoming a writer until I was twelve, though it was among the many occupations I had played at in earlier childhood. I should have liked to be an urban planner, but I discovered, before I had any opportunity to set out on such a path, that the profession had already become what it has since remained: not a branch of engineering in which one does the interesting creative work of coming up with feasible ways of giving people the kind of towns they want to live in, but a branch of politics in which one plans the kind of towns demanded by the ideology of one's superiors, and then crams them down the people's throats. I thought of being a cartographer – the maps in *National Geographic*, of all things, were nearly my first purely aesthetic experience – but I could not discover any path that would lead me appreciably in the direction of such a career. In any case my formal education was forcibly terminated before I could make any meaningful progress towards those ends.

But writing was something that I could (and can) do, and that nobody could *stop* me from doing so long as I lived in a relatively free country. In an age of galloping credentialism, when even security guards are examined and licensed by the State, there is to this day no formal credential for becoming a writer – no storyteller's certificate, not even a blogger's licence. It is true that the creative writing programs in the universities turn out more graduates than formerly, but so far the only people that have been thereby prevented from becoming creative writers are those very same graduates. Perhaps some of the reasons for this will eventually occur to them, or even to their professors. But I digress—

In Calgary, when I was still a fairly small boy, there was a sort of minor mania for local history that lasted several years. Southern Alberta was one of the last places in North America to be definitely settled. It was only in 1875 that the first permanent building was erected on the future site of the city. That was Fort Calgary, the North-West Mounted Police post, one of several built to shut down the illicit whisky trade out of the United States. The last survivors of the pioneer period, or rather the youngest of their children, were busily dying in the 1970s, and their stories being written up by local historians like Jack Peach and Grant MacEwan, themselves old men. I myself had a second or third cousin who was so old that he had come west by covered wagon, and lived to the age of 105; and my own grandfather took up a homestead on virgin land in the Peace River country about the time my father was born, not long before the arable land ran out and the homestead system was abolished.

It should come as no surprise that my first large creative endeavour sprang out of that environment and those vicarious experiences. Where the young C. S. Lewis (and his brother) had an imaginary country, Boxen, whose history and legends came to be written up in considerable detail, I had an imaginary frontier town. I drew many maps of the place at different periods, but also wrote portions of a connected history of the place and its leading citizens, leading down from the first settlers to the imaginary characters that I and one or two of my friends played at being in the present day. All that stuff was lost long ago, thank God; some of it I destroyed myself, but most was thrown away by my mother, who never saw a piece of paper that she did not detest on sight. The fact that my father was an avid reader and liked to fill up the house with books was, I believe, a constant anguish to her.

I had left that phase behind and was writing 'future history' and pastiches of bad science fiction when, at the age of twelve, I abruptly discovered that writing was something one could do as a profession. I have had no measurable success at it since then, but I still persist in trying: partly because one *can* earn money by it, even (nowadays, through the medium of ebooks) with very small sales, and it is one of the few kinds of work that I can do in my present state of health without expensive academic credentials; but chiefly for another reason. Since that reason has not, in my experience, been much talked about, I propose to say something about it here.

.Orwell, in the essay quoted above, suggested that there were four main reasons why people become writers:

> (i) *Sheer egoism*. Desire to seem clever, to be talked about, to be remembered after death, to get your own back on the grown-ups who snubbed you in childhood, etc., etc. It is humbug to

pretend this is not a motive, and a strong one. Writers share this characteristic with scientists, artists, politicians, lawyers, soldiers, successful businessmen – in short, with the whole top crust of humanity. The great mass of human beings are not acutely selfish. After the age of about thirty they almost abandon the sense of being individuals at all – and live chiefly for others, or are simply smothered under drudgery. But there is also the minority of gifted, willful people who are determined to live their own lives to the end, and writers belong in this class. Serious writers, I should say, are on the whole more vain and self-centred than journalists, though less interested in money.

(ii) Aesthetic enthusiasm. Perception of beauty in the external world, or, on the other hand, in words and their right arrangement. Pleasure in the impact of one sound on another, in the firmness of good prose or the rhythm of a good story. Desire to share an experience which one feels is valuable and ought not to be missed. The aesthetic motive is very feeble in a lot of writers, but even a pamphleteer or writer of textbooks will have pet words and phrases which appeal to him for non-utilitarian reasons; or he may feel strongly about typography, width of margins, etc. Above the level of a railway guide, no book is quite free from aesthetic considerations.

(iii) Historical impulse. Desire to see things as they are, to find out true facts and store them up for the use of posterity.

(iv) Political purpose. – Using the word 'political' in the widest possible sense. Desire to push the world in a certain direction, to alter other people's idea of the kind of society that they should strive after. Once again, no book is genuinely free from political bias. The opinion that art should have nothing to do with politics is itself a political attitude.

All four of these motives can be found in my own make-up, but besides these there is an item *(v)* without which I would never have persisted as long as I have, nor through such deserts of solitude and obscurity. I thought at first of calling it *social purpose,* but that sounds too much like the *political* purpose mentioned by Orwell; we have grown so accustomed to thinking that anything labelled 'social' must have something to do with socialism. Instead I shall describe it as *frustrated gregariousness.*

Like Orwell, I was a disagreeable child, and (as I now believe) imagined myself to be even worse than I was. I was quite shamelessly bullied at school, and shunned by children who were not themselves bullies: a wise precaution on their part, as my presence was liable to draw bullies to the neighbourhood. I had very few friends in childhood, and most of those were odd ducks and outcasts like myself. I did not even have an imaginary friend, as I have heard many lonely children do; the idea simply never occurred to me. But I did have books. My father had at least a thousand of them in the house, and I began to add to the number as soon as I had my own pocket-money. I hardly knew a human being who was interested in history, or science, or in the perplexing questions that I had not yet learnt to put under the heading of philosophy. But there was Will Durant, whose eleven fat volumes of world history took up almost a whole shelf of my father's biggest bookcase; and the *Life Science Library,* with volumes on every subject from *The Body* to *Wheels;* and the marvellous George Gamow, whom I did not yet know as the co-inventor of the Big Bang theory, but whose book *One Two Three ... Infinity* taught my mind to do cartwheels and handsprings (and count transfinite numbers); and many others.

Then there were the pure storytellers, beginning with Dr. Seuss and L. Frank Baum and A. A. Milne, soon followed by Bradbury and Heinlein and Kipling, the Whites (E. B. and T. H.), Lloyd Alexander, John Christopher with his *Tripods* series, and others less fantastical. Beverly Cleary's Henry Huggins and Keith Robertson's Henry Reed were two of my better friends in those days, though I never knew a Henry in real life. I liked and rather envied the Melendy family and their strange old house, the Four-Story Mistake; and the Gilbreths of *Cheaper By the Dozen,* who had the disadvantage of being real people (most of them were still living when I first read about them), but the glamour of distance and the patina of times past; and I found a kindred spirit in Meg Murry, and another, less well known, in the hero of a book called *Trillions*, by Nicholas Fisk. (His name was Scott, if I recall correctly, and he fought a doomed and desperate action against any and all attempts to call him Scotty: that alone won my heartfelt sympathy and commiseration.) And in due course, after I had been well prepared to appreciate them, there were J. R. R. Tolkien and C. S. Lewis.

Of course I wanted to talk about the things I had read, and of course (being the unlikable creature that I was) I had, for the most part, nobody to talk to. My father listened with patience and some understanding when he could, but he was busy and overworked; my mother was not the sort of person one could talk to about anything. And I was, in effect, an only child. I had a stepbrother, my mother's son by her long-ago first marriage, but he had left home when I was small, by the expedient of staying in Vancouver when the family moved to Calgary; and when we did meet we had little in common. There seemed nobody to talk to about my beloved books – *except the books themselves*. I was like a shipwrecked sailor who kept finding messages in bottles on the strand. Well, I could never hope to meet the far-sundered souls who sent the bottles, but I could write messages of my own and hope they would one day be found. In such a way, I thought, I could take some part in the great conversation, and have someone to talk to about the things I felt most deeply, the things that mattered and endured.

Like Orwell, I tried to give up writing for several years – in my case, from roughly the ages of 25 to 30 – and I, too, found that I was 'outraging my true nature'. It was Dave Duncan who talked me out of writing; he assured me, with the grand depressive *gravitas* that only a Presbyterian Scotsman can produce at will, that *he* belonged to the last generation of writers – that literature itself was obsolete, that he should retire in a few years and there would be no more readers or writers thereafter. Orwell spent his years of exile in the Indian Imperial Police; my own were passed in less salubrious activities and less respectable places, but they served me, in their way, as the same kind of education in the varieties of human nature. Eventually my business and my ill-starred common-law coupling both collapsed; I retooled and came back online as a writer, though with no greater success than I had found in my futile early twenties. About this time a woman named Rowling began to be heard of: Dave Duncan's prophecy had been slightly premature.

I have had little enough success in the years since then. The obvious explanation is that I cannot write, or at least not well enough to please an audience. This idea has occurred to me, but I find that it does not quite adequately cover the facts. There is a story about Fred Astaire. Once when he was working on a film, going through take after take in a futile attempt to capture a flawless performance, he left the sound stage at the end of the day, flung a tragic arm round Alan Jay Lerner's shoulder, and cried out: 'Oh, Alan, why doesn't someone tell me that I cannot dance?' I keep looking for someone who will tell me that I cannot write, and so far I have not found anyone but myself; and what do I know? But neither have I the knack of getting my work before any appreciable audience. Hence my running joke about my 3.6 Loyal Readers, a number that has been hallowed by tradition and shall never be changed, though the actual number of my readers may now be somewhat larger and is (in all probability) an integer.

But it is not for the 3.6, or however many of you there are, that I write; I say it with apologies, and meaning no disrespect. I write for the Great Conversation; because I met most of my friends in books, the friends that kept me alive and (reasonably) sane through my friendless years, and it is only in the same medium that I can talk back to them and tell them what they have meant to me. In practical terms the debt can never be paid back, because most of the authors I read in my youth are dead now, and the others are cut off from me by chasms of fame and accomplishment, as inaccessible as the moon since Apollo discontinued his passenger service.

But perhaps a little of it can be paid forward. Perhaps some day, somewhere, another lonely soul, or even a lonely child, will pick up one of my books and find a friend, a few hours of consolation, a word of encouragement or even wisdom in the solitary struggle to stay alive and human. It would gratify me, I suppose, if it happened in my lifetime and

I got to hear of it. But one does not write for that kind of gratification; people who *need* that reward seek it in other places – this business, even in the best of cases, pays too slowly for that to be an effectual motive. (L. Frank Baum, for instance, had been dead fifty years when I was born.) My one constant desire through the years has been to light a candle of my own in honour of the stars that have shone upon me, and hope that someone will see it, and that some measure of the darkness will be lifted from his eyes.

WORKS CITED

Aldiss, Brian. *Report on Probability A*. London: Faber and Faber, 1968.

Alexander, Samuel. *Space, Time, and Deity*. London: Macmillan, 1920.

Asimov, Isaac. *I. Asimov: A Memoir*. New York: Doubleday, 1994.

Fowler, H. W. *A Dictionary of Modern English Usage*, 1st ed. Oxford: Oxford University Press, 1926.

Frost, Robert. 'The Figure A Poem Makes'. Text online at http://www.mrbauld.com/frostfig.html

Heinlein, Robert A. *Grumbles From the Grave*. New York: Del Rey, 1989.

—*Stranger in a Strange Land*. New York: Putnam, 1961.

—'On the Writing of Speculative Fiction'. In *Of Worlds Beyond: The Science of Science Fiction Writing*, ed. Lloyd Arthur Eshbach. Chicago: Advent, 1964.

Johnson, Paul. *The Birth of the Modern: World Society 1815–1830*. New York: HarperCollins, 1991.

Key, Keegan-Michael, and Jordan Peele. *Key & Peele* (TV series). Comedy Central, 2012.

Kipling, Rudyard. *Something of Myself: For My Friends Known and Unknown*. London: Macmillan, 1937.

Le Guin, Ursula K. *The Language of the Night*. New York: Putnam, 1979.

Lewis, C. S. *Surprised by Joy*. London: Geoffrey Bles, 1955.

Marzán, Julio. *The Spanish American Roots of William Carlos Williams.* Austin: University of Texas Press, 1994.

McGrath, Scott. 'Hard Work *vs.* Working Hard'. Retrieved from https://web.archive.org/web/20120416231632/http://www.scottmcgrath.ca/coaching-corner/hard-work-vs-working-hard/

Miller, Laura. 'Sentenced to death'. *Salon,* August 2001. Text online at http://www.salon.com/2001/08/16/novels/

Myers, B. R. *A Reader's Manifesto.* New York: Melville House, 2002. An abridged version was published as an article in *The Atlantic,* July/August 2001. Abridged text online at http://www.theatlantic.com/magazine/archive/2001/07/a-readers-manifesto/302270/

Orwell, George. 'Inside the Whale'. *Inside the Whale and Other Essays.* London: Victor Gollancz, 1940.

—*Keep the Aspidistra Flying.* London: Victor Gollancz, 1936.

—'Why I Write'. In *Gangrel,* Summer 1946. Text online at http://orwell.ru/library/essays/wiw/english/e_wiw

Polti, Georges. *The Thirty-six Dramatic Situations.*

Proulx, Annie. *Accordion Crimes.* New York: Scribners, 1996.

Robinson, Spider. 'The Reference Library' (column), in *Analog Science Fiction/Science Fact,* February 1978.

Sayre, Henry M. *The Visual Text of William Carlos Williams.* Champaign: University of Illinois Press, 1983.

Shakespeare, William. *Macbeth.* London: Edward Blount, 1623 (and innumerable other editions).

Smith, Dean Wesley. 'Killing the Sacred Cows of Publishing: Writers Compete With Each Other'. Text online at http://www.deanwesleysmith.com/killing-the-sacred-cows-of-publishing-writers-compete-with-each-other/

Sturgeon, Theodore. Book review in *Venture Science Fiction,* Sept. 1957.

Theis, Jim. 'The Eye of Argon'. Originally published in OSFAN, the journal of the Ozark SF Fan Society, No. 10. Facsimile of the original apazine online at http://ansible.uk/misc/eyeargon.pdf

Wasserman, Steve. 'The Amazon Effect'. *The Nation,* May 29, 2012. Text online at http://www.thenation.com/article/amazon-effect/

Wolverton, Dave. 'On Writing as a Fantasist'. *Tangent* #18, Spring 1997. Retrieved from http://www.tangentonline.com/articles-columnsmenu-284/529-on-writing-as-a-fantasist

Specific references by chapter

Style is the rocket

'In certain genres': Wasserman, 'The Amazon Effect'.

'The sentence cult': Myers, *passim.*

'Much of "A Reader's Manifesto" is wasted': Miller, 'Sentenced to death'.

'In "cultured" circles': Orwell, 'Inside the Whale'.

'I can see that it will go *round*': Johnson, *The Birth of the Modern,* 612.

'Wonderfully as he can describe an *appearance*': Orwell, 'Inside the Whale'.

'Contemplation and enjoyment': Alexander, *Space, Time, and Deity.* I am indebted to C. S. Lewis's summary in *Surprised by Joy,* chapter 14.

'Lawrence was all right': Orwell, *Keep the Aspidistra Flying,* chapter 1.

'She stood there, amazed, rooted': Proulx, *Accordion Crimes,* 370.

'The last thing Proulx wants': Myers.

'There is no *is* without it': Le Guin, 'From Elfland to Poughkeepsie', in *Language of the Night.*

The drudge and the architect

'Working hard doesn't mean you're doing hard work': McGrath, 'Hard Work *vs.* Working Hard'.

'For me, knowing I'm doing': *Ibid.*

The immersive writer

'I have learned two ways': Heinlein, *Stranger,* chapter 12.

'No tears in the writer': Frost, 'The Figure A Poem Makes'.

'Open mode' and 'closed mode': Cleese, SMI talk.

'I was always intrigued': *Ibid.*

Sturgeon's Law School
'Ninety percent of science fiction is crud': Sturgeon, *Venture*.
'The weather beaten trail': Theis, 'The Eye of Argon'.

Quality *vs* quality
'O hell-kite! – All?': Shakespeare, *Macbeth*, act IV, scene 3.

Ozamataz
'T. J. Juckson', 'Hingle McCringleberry', *etc.*: *Key & Peele,* episode 10, 'East-West Collegiate Bowl'.

The Emperor's new prose
'Considering how cerebral our genre is': Robinson, in *Analog*, February 1978.
'There is indeed a certain charm': Fowler, 'Irrelevant Allusion', in *Modern English Usage*, 297.
'The realist movement quickly developed a trend toward elitism': Wolverton.
'To arrive at "The Red Wheelbarrow"': Marzán, 161.
'It is crucial that Williams's material is banal': Sayre, 66.
'Similar elitist fiction': Wolverton, *op. cit.*
'At present the face was in movement' (and subsequent quotations): Aldiss.

Heinlein's rules and Amazon's game
'1. You must write': Heinlein, 'On the Writing of Speculative Fiction'.
'I am tempted to type those excess eighty-three words': Heinlein, *Grumbles From the Grave*, 232.
'This leads me to the Higher Editing': Kipling, *Something of Myself.* Chapter VIII, 'Working Tools'.
'I forget who started the notion': *Ibid.*
'When I was handing out Hugos': Asimov, chapter 81.

Clock share: Writers *vs.* the competition
'The myth is simply that writers compete': Smith.
'So, let me take a hard look at the reality': *Ibid.*

Why I write
'I was the middle child of three': Orwell, 'Why I Write'.
'(i) Sheer egoism': *Ibid.*

ABOUT THE AUTHOR

Tom Simon was a small child at the time of the first Moon landing, and like many small children at that time, he wanted to grow up to be an astronaut. This desire led him to the first momentous decision of his life. His father was six feet tall, and he wanted to be taller than that; but since NASA set a maximum height of 6′3″ for astronauts, not *too* much taller. He therefore decided to grow to 6′2½″, to allow a margin for error. This was the first and last time that something in his life worked out exactly according to plan.

The shocking neglect of manned space flight after the end of the Apollo program robbed young Mr. Simon of his first ambition, so he was forced to seek another vocation. (He was also left in a state of being tall for no particular purpose.) If he could not travel in space himself, he could at least write about it; and so he concluded to become a science fiction writer. Along the way, he discovered that his *métier* was really for epic fantasy (and the odd spot of criticism), and he has persevered at that, in a fitful way, ever since. Still, his early love for rockets remains with him, along with his later taste for style in writing; and sometimes they combine, as in the title of this book.

Made in the USA
Lexington, KY
23 December 2016